CRITICAL
ANTHOLOGIES OF
NONFICTION
WRITING™

CRITICAL PERSPECTIVES ON AL QAEDA

Edited by
April Isaacs

THE ROSEN PUBLISHING GROUP, INC.
NEW YORK

Published in 2006 by The Rosen Publishing Group, Inc.
29 East 21st Street, New York, NY 10010

First Edition

Library of Congress Cataloging-in-Publication Data

Critical perspectives on Al Qaeda / edited by April Isaacs.
    p. cm.—(Critical anthologies of nonfiction writing)
Includes bibliographical references and index.
ISBN 1-4042-0542-X (library binding)
1. Qaida (Organization) 2. Terrorism.
I. Isaacs, April. II. Series.
HV6432.5.Q2C75 2006
303.6'25—dc22

                                        2005012464

Manufactured in the United States of America

On the cover: Ayman al-Zawahiri, Al Qaeda's second in command, appears on the Aljazeera television network on September 9, 2004.

CONTENTS

INTRODUCTION

In 1979, Osama bin Laden graduated from college with a degree in civil engineering. College had been a formative experience for the young man from Saudi Arabia. In addition to the knowledge gained from the school's engineering curriculum, he cultivated a passionate faith in Islam, the religion of 1.5 billion Muslims around the world.

Upon graduation, he walked into a world that was rife with conflict. Two superpowers, the United States and the Soviet Union, were in the middle of the Cold War. The Soviets were struggling to maintain power and influence over communist states on the verge of overthrowing their governments. One such nation was Afghanistan, which had been invaded by the Soviets in December 1979. Several nations, including the United States, funneled in money to support the Afghan cause. Muslim warriors from around the world came to Afghanistan to join their fellow Muslims in the fight against the Soviets. These dedicated warriors inspired bin Laden, who admired their bravery and loyalty to Islam. Alongside his college mentor, a man named Abdullah Azzam, he founded a resistance group that funded, trained, and organized troops to resist the Soviet invasion.

At the time, most of the world had never heard of Osama bin Laden, nor did they know the extent or importance of the war that was being waged on the mountainous terrain of a troubled Afghanistan. However, this would prove to be one of the most influential events of the twentieth century. A number of the warriors who fought the Soviets would disperse and regroup into an organization the entire world would come to know on the fateful day of September 11, 2001. Bin Laden, their leader, would be regarded throughout much of the world as a ruthless terrorist and the most wanted man in America.

After the war in Afghanistan, the resistance fighters (known as the mujahideen) broke into several different groups. The group led by Osama bin Laden became known as Al Qaeda, which means "the base" in Arabic. Osama bin Laden returned home to Saudi Arabia, where a new conflict was beginning—the Gulf War (1990–1991). He urged the Saudi government to let him call the mujahideen to arms to protect the holy lands of Medina and Mecca. However, the Saudi government rejected bin Laden's assistance. The mujahideen were viewed throughout parts of the Middle East as rogues who could only impair a nation's relationship with Western countries such as the United States.

Bin Laden was enraged when the Saudis allowed U.S. troops to station themselves in Saudi Arabia. In bin Laden's opinion, this violated a tenet of Islam that no two religions should exist in the Holy Land. Bin Laden's fury and proclamations against the Saudi government eventually got him expelled from the country. He sought refuge in the African country of Sudan.

In 1996, bin Laden returned to Afghanistan where a new governing body had taken over the country. The group was called the Taliban and bin Laden quickly forged a relationship with its leader, Mullah Mohammed Omar. Bin Laden established Afghanistan as the home base for Al Qaeda and its leadership.

With the protection of the Taliban, bin Laden was able to plan and execute one of history's most heinous acts of terrorism.

On September 11, 2001, the world changed forever when two hijacked commercial planes crashed into the World Trade Center in New York City. A third crashed into the Pentagon, and a fourth crashed in a field in Pennsylvania (but was most likely headed for the White House). Al Qaeda and its leader, Osama bin Laden, were the primary suspects. Since the attacks, U.S. foreign policy has taken some drastic turns. The United States entered Afghanistan, ousted the oppressive Taliban government that was harboring Al Qaeda, started a global war on terror, apprehended several key members of Al Qaeda's network, and invaded Iraq.

The September 11 terrorist attack was not the first time the United States had been attacked by Al Qaeda. The first major terrorist attack against the United States by Al Qaeda was the 1998 bombing of two East African U.S. embassies, one in Nairobi, Kenya, and one in Dar es Salaam, Tanzania. Al Qaeda has also been named responsible for terrorist attacks against citizens of other nations after September 11, 2001. These attacks include the 2004 train bombings in Madrid, Spain, and the 2002 nightclub bombing in Bali, Indonesia, which was in partnership with another militant Islamic terrorist organization, Jemaah Islamiah.

Just as the United States has changed dramatically since 9/11, so has the Al Qaeda network. Though many of its members have been captured, several still remain at large, including Osama bin Laden and his trusted deputy and second in command, Ayman al-Zawahiri. Al Qaeda is no longer clearly confined to one ideology or one region. It is far reaching, and it encompasses terrorist groups that may differ in many ways but are united in their animosity toward America and its foreign policy. Such a vague and widespread organization, inspired by the events of September 11, 2001, has proven to be a formidable, elusive, and at times indefinable foe.

This anthology will provide a study of Al Qaeda through twenty-two vital pieces of writing on the subject from the past decade. The articles have been selected to include diverse opinions and have been culled from a range of materials, including newspapers, magazines, books, and Web sites. Within these articles, you'll learn more about the men behind Al Qaeda, the roots of the organization, and the world's response to the group's acts of terror. *—AI*

CHAPTER ONE

TIME, CONTINUITY, AND CHANGE: AL QAEDA'S PAST, PRESENT, AND FUTURE

The roots of Al Qaeda go back to the Soviet invasion of Afghanistan in 1979, when a group of warriors called the mujahideen descended upon Afghanistan to battle the Soviets. Bin Laden was one of their chief organizers and sources of funding. The mujahideen also received financial support from other sources, among them the United States, which was in conflict with the Soviet Empire.

Considered the bloodiest yet most successful jihad (Islamic holy war) in modern times, the decade-long battle received little media attention. Yet the victories achieved in Afghanistan bolstered bin Laden, who would later transform the mujahideen into ministers of a new terrorist organization—Al Qaeda.

As a reporter for CNN, *Peter Bergen began researching and writing his book* Holy War, Inc. *several years before September 11, 2001. The book's publication shortly after 9/11 was timely and offered remarkable historical insight into the origins of Al Qaeda to a public stunned, angry, and in mourning. This excerpt details the origins of the mujahideen as well as bin Laden's early life as a radical Islamist. —AI*

From *Holy War, Inc.*
by Peter Bergen
2001

[1979] was the dawn of a new century in the Muslim calendar, traditionally a time of change. And what changes there were. In January the Shah of Iran was overthrown and the Ayatollah Khomeini returned to Tehran. Then, in March, to the consternation of many Muslims, Egypt and Israel signed a peace deal. In November came the shocking news that hundreds of armed Islamist militants had seized Islam's holy of holies, the Grand Mosque in Mecca, and engaged in a days-long bloody battle with security forces that left hundreds dead and dealt a severe blow to the prestige of the House of Saud. Finally, in late December, the Soviets invaded Afghanistan. This was arguably the most earthshaking news of all: the godless communists had taken a sovereign Muslim nation by force.

The invasion was an event of signal importance for the West. President Carter, who had previously taken an accommodationist approach with the Soviets, now espoused a hard line. But its loudest echo was in the Muslim world. Just as in the 1930s an international cast of liberals and socialists—men like George Orwell, Ernest Hemingway, and John Dos Passos—were drawn to Spain to the war against Franco's Fascists, so Muslims from around the globe were drawn to fight the USSR in the Afghan war in the 1980s.

The Soviet war in Afghanistan was one of the most brutal wars of our brutal era. The Russians killed over a million people and forced about five million, a third of the country, into exile. It was also one of the most significant conflicts since World War II, giving the lie to the might of the Soviet military machine. Paradoxically it was also one of the most underreported wars of past decades. As the historian Robert D. Kaplan has pointed out, at least ten times more people died in Afghanistan than in the civil wars that started in Lebanon in 1975, yet "Afghanistan, which on the scale of suffering vastly overshadowed any other military conflict of the 1980s was, quite simply, almost unconsciously ignored."

This was not surprising. Journalists who went into Afghanistan had to endure weeks of walking over some of the most difficult terrain in the world, in constant fear of being attacked by helicopter gunships, eating rice if they were lucky, and exposing themselves to a wide range of unpleasant diseases. During the Vietnam war, by contrast, a porter could go to the front lines in a U.S. helicopter and be back at the hotel swimming pool later the same day, sipping a cold one. This is not to denigrate the many brave reporters in Vietnam, but simply to say that for those covering the Afghan war the risks were orders of magnitude higher, and the interest of news editors orders of magnitude lower, since no American soldiers' lives were at stake.

The journalist Rob Schultheis was one of the admirable few who repeatedly traveled inside Afghanistan. He described it as "the holiest of wars," and memorably wrote: "Those hopelessly brave warriors I walked with, and their families, who suffered so much for faith and freedom and who are still not free, they were truly the people of God."

Indeed, if any conflict deserved to be called a just jihad, the war against the Soviets in Afghanistan surely was. Unprovoked, a superpower invaded a largely peasant nation and inflicted on it a total, totalitarian war. The population rose up under the banner of Islam to drive the infidels out. In a 1985 report, an independent human rights organization summed up the Russians' unforgiving approach: "The Soviet air force is bombing populated areas . . . killing uncounted numbers of villagers. Soviet ground forces, now reinforced by specialized commando units have carried out even larger indiscriminate massacres. The Soviets continue to scatter anti-personnel mines in inhabited areas." Afghanistan would become one of the most heavily mined countries in the world.

. . . Within weeks of the Soviet invasion, bin Laden, then twenty-two, voted with his feet and wallet, heading to Pakistan to meet with the Afghan leaders Burhanuddin Rabbani and Abdul Rasool Sayyaf, whom he had previously encountered during Hajj gatherings. He then returned to Saudi Arabia and started lobbying his family and friends to provide money to support the mujahideen and continued making short trips to Pakistan for his fund-raising work.

In the early 1980s bin Laden, already an expert in demolition from time spent working in his family's construction business, made his first trips into Afghanistan, bringing with him hundreds of tons of construction machinery, bulldozers, loaders, dump trucks, and equipment for building trenches, which he put at the disposal of the mujahideen. The machinery would be used to build rough roads, dig tunnels into the mountains for shelter, and construct rudimentary hospitals. Bin Laden's followers also set up mine-sweeping operations in the Afghan countryside.

Despite the fact that the United States was also supporting the mujahideen, bin Laden was already voicing anti-American sentiments during the early eighties. Khaled al-Fawwaz, bin Laden's London contact, recalls his friend saying in 1982 that Muslims should boycott American products. In a 1999 interview, bin Laden himself said that during the mid-1980s he gave lectures in Saudi Arabia urging attacks on U.S. forces and the boycott of American products.

In 1984 bin Laden set up a guesthouse in Peshawar for Muslims drawn to the jihad. It was called Beit al-Ansar, or House of the Supporters, an allusion to the Prophet Muhammad's followers who helped him when he had to flee his native Mecca for Medina. Initially the house was simply a way station for those who would be sent for training with one of the Afghan factions. Later, bin Laden would form his own military operation. At about the time bin Laden founded Beit al-Ansar, his former professor Abdullah Azzam established the Mekhtab al-Khadamat, or Services Office, in Peshawar. The Services Office started publishing reports about the Afghan war and engaged in a global campaign to recruit Muslims for the jihad. Bin Laden was its principal funder. Eventually there would be a dozen or so guesthouses in Peshawar under the aegis of the Services Office.

Azzam was both the ideological godfather and the global recruiter par excellence of Muslims drawn to the Afghan jihad; he would exert a strong pull on bin Laden by virtue of his Islamic credentials and greater experience of the world. According to the Palestinian journalist Jamal Ismail, who was a student in Peshawar during the 1980s and met with bin Laden repeatedly after 1984: "It was Azzam who influenced Osama to finance the Arab fighters who came to Afghanistan." In an interview with an Arabic-language television station, bin Laden himself describes Azzam as a "man worth a nation." Those who knew Azzam and bin Laden during this period recall that while Azzam was eloquent and charismatic, bin Laden, then in his mid-twenties, seemed sincere and honest but not a potential leader.

. . . To understand the impact that Azzam had on bin Laden, and the whole of the subsequent jihadist movement, allow me a brief detour here to trace Azzam's life. Abdullah Azzam was born in a village in Palestine in 1941, near Jenin. He graduated with a degree in theology from Damascus University in 1966. Already a firm believer in jihad, and a passionate hater of Israelis, whom he blamed for taking Palestinian land to create their own state in 1948, Azzam fought them in the 1967 war. Afterward, he studied at al-Azhar University in Cairo, the preeminent center of Islamic thought. There he received first a master's degree and later, in 1973, a doctorate in Islamic jurisprudence. While studying in Cairo, Azzam befriended the family of the jihad ideologue Sayyid Qutb. Studying at al-Azhar at the same time as Azzam was the Egyptian Sheik Omar Abdel Rahman, later the spiritual leader of the jihadist movement in Egypt and a close colleague of Azzam's in the effort to create an international network of holy warriors during the 1980s.

. . . A barrel-chested man whose enormous gray beard and fiery rhetoric made him a commanding presence, Azzam believed that jihad was an absolute necessity to restore the Khalifa, the dream that Muslims around the world could be united under one ruler. His motto was "Jihad and the rifle alone: no negotiations, no conferences and no dialogues."

And he put that belief in practice, often joining the mujahideen battling the Soviets in Afghanistan.

For Azzam the jihad in Afghanistan was an obligation for every Muslim, as he explained in a widely distributed pamphlet entitled "Defending Muslim Territory Is the Most Important Duty." And it was not simply from Afghanistan that the infidels had to be expelled. Azzam wrote: "This duty will not end with victory in Afghanistan; jihad will remain an individual obligation until all other lands that were Muslim are returned to us so that Islam will reign again: before us lie Palestine, Bokhara, Lebanon, Chad, Eritrea, Somalia, the Philippines, Burma, Southern Yemen, Tashkent and Andalusia [southern Spain]."

Azzam traveled all over the world to recruit men and money for the Afghan jihad, preaching that "to stand one hour in the battle line in the cause of Allah is better than sixty years of night prayer." Khaled al-Fawwaz recalls that Azzam was a one-man "wire service" for the jihad movement, traveling to Kuwait, Yemen, Bahrain, Saudi Arabia, and the United States to gather and spread news, recruit men, and raise millions of dollars for the cause.

The power of Azzam's message was so strong that even via the medium of videotape observant Muslims felt the pull of his call to holy war. Mohamed Odeh, a Jordanian citizen of Palestinian descent who would play a role in the 1998 bombing of the American embassy in Kenya, was a student of engineering in the Philippines in the late eighties, when he watched a video by Azzam extolling the Afghan jihad. Odeh soon traveled to Afghanistan, where he was trained in the use of a wide variety of weapons, including AK-47s, machine guns, and antitank and antiaircraft missiles, and of explosives such as C3, C4, and TNT. He also subsequently swore an oath of allegiance to bin Laden.

. . . Another influential figure in the Arab effort to support the war was Muhammad Abdurrahman Khalifa, a Jordanian, who would later go on to marry one of bin Laden's sisters. Khalifa headed the Jordanian branch of the Muslim Brotherhood, which supplied recruits for the Afghan jihad. Khalifa also worked in Peshawar as head of the Saudi Muslim World League office during the Afghan jihad.

Meanwhile, bin Laden traveled back and forth to Saudi Arabia, bringing donations for various Afghan parties, including that of the military commander Ahmad Shah Massoud, a moderate Islamist. But bin Laden would form his closest ties with the ultra-Islamist Hekmatyar and with Sayyaf, an Afghan leader who was fluent in Arabic and had studied in Saudi Arabia. Sayyaf also subscribed to the purist Wahhabi Islam dear to bin Laden's heart. Because of his close ties to Arabia, Sayyaf would receive hundreds of millions of dollars in Saudi aid.

. . . With the establishment of the Services Office by Azzam and bin Laden in 1984, Arab support for the mujahideen became more overt. The recruits for the Afghan jihad came to be known as the Afghan Arabs. None of them was Afghan, and while most were Arabs, they also came from all over the Muslim world. Some of them were high school students who went on trips to the Afghan-Pakistan border that were not much more than the equivalent of jihad summer camp. Some were involved in support operations along the border, working for charities and hospitals. Others spent years in fierce battles against the communists.

According to Jamal Ismail, three countries provided the lion's share of the Afghan Arabs: Saudi Arabia, Yemen, and Algeria. Saudi Arabia's national airline even gave a 75 percent discount to those going to the holy war. By Ismail's account, fifty thousand Arabs came to Peshawar to fight. Bin Laden's friend Khaled al-Fawwaz told me the figure was 25,000. Milt Bearden, who ran the CIAs Afghan operation between 1986 and 1989, also puts the figure at 25,000. No one really knows the exact figure, but it seems safe to say that the total number of Afghan Arabs who participated in the jihad over the course of the entire war was in the low tens of thousands.

It is worth noting here that the maximum combined strengths of the various Afghan mujahideen factions averaged somewhere between 175,000 and 250,000 in any given year. These numbers demonstrate that the Afghan Arabs' contribution to the war against the Soviets was insignificant from a military point of view. The war was won primarily with the blood of Afghans and secondarily with the treasure of the United States and Saudi Arabia, who between them provided approximately $6 billion in support.

. . . In the grand scheme of things the Afghan Arabs were no more than extras in the Afghan holy war. It was the lessons they learned from the jihad, rather than their contribution to it, that proved significant. They rubbed shoulders with militants from dozens of countries and were indoctrinated in the most extreme ideas concerning jihad. They received at least some sort of military training, and in some cases battle-field experience. Those who had had their tickets punched in the Afghan conflict went back to their home countries with the ultimate credential for later holy wars. And they believed that their exertions had defeated a superpower. "The Afghan jihad plays a central role in the evolution of the Islamist movement around the world," writes Gilles Kepel, a scholar of militant Islam. "It replaces the Palestinian cause in the Arab imagination, and symbolizes the movement from [Arab] nationalism to Islamism."

Jawal Ismail recalls that by about December 1984, bin Laden had become an important figure in the jihad effort. Around this time Azzam announced that bin Laden would pay the living expenses of the families of men who came to fight in the Afghan war. Since Pakistan was inexpensive, that sum was about $300 a month per family. Still, it added up. According to Essam Deraz, a filmmaker who covered bin Laden in the late 1980s, the Saudi was subsidizing the Afghan Arabs at a rate of $25,000 a month during this period. Bin Laden's friend al-Fawwaz said bin Laden also started thinking about how he could create a mobile force. "He bought four-wheel-drive pickups and equipped every one with antitank missiles and mine detection so that each unit would be capable of dealing with any kind of situation," recounted al-Fawwaz.

In 1986 bin Laden moved to Peshawar permanently, directing his operation from a two-story villa in the suburb of University Town where he both worked and lived. It was at this time that bin Laden founded his first camp inside Afghanistan, named al-Ansar, near the village of Jaji in Paktia province, a few miles from a portion of Pakistan's North-West Frontier that juts into Afghanistan. At Jaji, bin Laden and his men would receive their baptism by fire: a week-long siege by the Soviets that has become a cornerstone of the popular legend surrounding bin Laden.

According to Deraz, who said he witnessed the battle of Jaji from a distance of about two miles, the Soviet assault began on April 17, 1987. The Arabs had based themselves at Jaji because it was close to the Soviet front lines, and had used bin Laden's construction equipment to dig themselves into caves in the heights around the village. For about a week they endured punishing bombardment by the two hundred-odd Russians, some of whom were wearing the uniform of Spetsnaz, Russia's special forces. Of about fifty Arabs, more than a dozen were killed before the group realized they could no longer hold their position and withdrew.

Despite this retreat, Jaji was celebrated as a victory in the Arab world. It was the first time the Afghan Arabs had held their ground for any length of time against such superior forces. Arab journalists based in Peshawar wrote daily dispatches about bin Laden's battlefield exploits that were widely published in the Middle East and brought a flood of new recruits to the Afghan jihad. Osama the lion was lionized for leaving behind the typical Saudi multimillionaire's life of palaces in Jeddah and hotel suites in London and Monte Carlo for the dangers of the war in Afghanistan. This was in sharp contrast to the thousands of members of the al-Saud ruling family, none of whom seem to have fought in Afghanistan despite awarding themselves the title of "Custodians" of Islam's holiest sites in 1986.

———■———

On September 11, 2001, when a hijacked plane flew into one of the World Trade Center towers, it first seemed like a horrible accident. Then, a second plane hit the other tower, and it became clear that the United States had been attacked by terrorists. But who was the perpetrator? The nation was almost too wounded and shocked to contemplate the person or people behind such an atrocity. Phone lines were down, thousands of people were missing, the downtown area of Manhattan had been completely evacuated, and every day the death toll climbed, as relief workers sifted through the rubble.

However, almost immediately after the attacks, the United States had a large-scale investigation under way. The following article, written three days after the tragedy, details the investigation and acknowledges bin Laden as a possible suspect. Upon further inquiries, the United States would later name bin Laden as the primary suspect. Three years later, bin Laden himself would admit full responsibility for 9/11. —AI

"Going After the Bad Guys"
by Kevin Whitelaw
U.S. News and World Report, September 14, 2001

The detective work has begun. Buried in the flight manifest of one of the doomed airliners, investigators have discovered names of people they believe are linked to al-Qaeda, the shadowy network of Islamic terrorists headed by Saudi exile Osama bin Laden.

The clue on the passenger list is just one of hundreds of bits of evidence and tips the FBI is following up in what Attorney General John Ashcroft called perhaps the most massive investigation in American history. But even before the first evidence surfaced, bin Laden topped suspect lists. The coordinated, comprehensive, and ruthless attack bears the trademark of the hunted terrorist, who from remote camps in the mountains of Afghanistan had vowed just three weeks ago to carry out an "unprecedented" attack against American interests.

It was a boast American officials had to take seriously. Bin Laden's operatives had already demonstrated their skill and dedication three years ago when they launched two nearly simultaneous bombings of U.S. embassies in Africa, as well as last year's suicide assault against an American warship, the USS *Cole*. Still, the incredible feat of hijacking four airliners and striking at two symbols of American power—its money and military might—astonished even veteran counterterrorism experts. "They've probably tested this many times," says Robert Blitzer, former head of domestic terrorism for the FBI. "It was an absolutely brilliant attack."

Yet the attackers left footprints that federal officials are confident will be tracked back to the source. Eavesdroppers at the National Security Agency scrambled in the hours after to monitor phone calls, faxes, or E-mails that might contain messages of congratulations from members of the terrorist groups. Quickly, operators intercepted a phone call between two known associates of bin Laden; they were heard talking about hitting two targets.

The FBI, meanwhile, has 7,000 special agents and support personnel on the case and is reviewing the passenger manifests, rental car receipts, telephone logs, and even videotapes from parking garages and pay phones. Investigators are also searching for the black boxes of the planes, which may contain recordings of the last cockpit conversations. Besides identifying the hijackers, authorities are tracking down accomplices who might still pose a threat to America's air system. Indeed, there is still concern that other terrorist acts are possible. "The U.S. is not fully confident it is done," says a counterterrorism official.

The aggressive investigation is producing leads, and fast: Authorities in Boston identified five Arab men as suspects and seized a rental car; inside they found an Arabic-language flight training manual. In Florida, federal agents searched numerous homes and businesses in connection with the investigation.

Blame Game

Though most intelligence sources seem convinced that bin Laden's operatives are behind the attack, the administration has been careful not to accuse him publicly. U.S. officials caution that evidence might show that other groups, perhaps Lebanon's Hezbollah, acted independently to stage the attack. Investigators are also looking hard at Algerian terrorists, who are tied to several millennium terrorist attempts. In 1994, an Algerian cell hijacked an Air France jet and threatened to blow it up over Paris.

It is the precision of this week's operation and its destructiveness that are steering authorities toward bin Laden as the prime culprit. "There is no other group or individual calling for coordinated attacks on the United States," says Larry Johnson, former deputy chief of the State Department's counterterrorism office. For example, bin Laden's followers had the ability to commandeer and fly commercial jets. *U.S. News* has learned that American intelligence officials had advance knowledge that al-Qaeda was recruiting and training pilots. Attorney General Ashcroft confirms that some of them received pilot training in the United States. Two suspects attended five-month courses at a Florida flight school at a cost of $10,000 apiece, according to its owner, Rudi Dekkers of Huffman Aviation.

The man who has built this terror empire remains hidden on secret bases scattered throughout Afghanistan, where he finances and inspires a vast, but loose, web of terrorist groups, from Egyptian Islamic Jihad to Abu Sayyaf in the Philippines. Cells have been identified in some 50 countries around the world—and if the FBI dragnet is correct, some of the cells are in unlikely American locales such as Portland, Maine, and South Florida. Bin Laden does not command his disciples so much as he helps facilitate their planning.

If bin Laden's al-Qaeda is behind this week's attack, officials will want to know whether the group got help, too. An operation like this one takes money, phony travel papers, and training—the sort of support that could be had from rogue states like Iraq or Afghanistan. A senior official tells *U.S. News* that Washington is looking at more than one—and as many as 10—countries that may be supporting groups linked to al-Qaeda.

State Sponsors

The first regime that may find itself in America's cross hairs is the hard-line Taliban regime in Afghanistan, which has given bin Laden safe harbor for the past five years. Taliban officials—and bin Laden himself—deny that the Saudi millionaire is involved in this week's strikes, but President Bush has already put them on notice, saying that America will make no distinction between terrorists and those who "harbor" them. The United States struck Afghanistan once before, with a pinprick cruise missile attack against bin Laden's training camps following the 1998 embassy bombings. But targeting other states could be more problematic if evidence linked them to the attack. U.S. experts are even looking at whether likely suspects such as Iraq's Saddam Hussein cooperated on the attack.

Amid cries of a new Pearl Harbor, the finger-pointing has already begun. "We have a major intelligence failure here," says Vincent Cannistraro, a former CIA counterterrorism chief. "To be caught completely with our pants down, it is just unbelievable." As spy agencies review weeks of intercepted phone calls and reports from field agents, they are likely to discover missed signals.

Indeed, in the weeks before the attack, U.S. officials were concerned about a possible terrorist attack, but their attention was focused on overseas targets. "That assumption may have had a distorting effect on how information was interpreted," says one senior U.S. source. Just last week, the State Department issued a new warning about an alert concerning U.S. forces in South Korea and Japan. And a senior U.S. official says that the government has been worried in recent days about an attack on U.S. interests in the Persian Gulf region.

The day before the attack on the Trade Center, two senior U.S. specialists—State Department counterterrorism director Francis Taylor and Defense Department terrorism official Austin Yamada—canceled planned trips abroad. The Pentagon denied any knowledge of Yamada's trip. U.S. officials insisted the Taylor cancellation was unrelated to any threat warning, but others say tensions were running high.

It is perhaps unfair to blame the intelligence community for failing to see the future, though it is precisely to prevent such catastrophes that the U.S. government spends $28 billion annually on spies and satellites. In their defense, U.S. intelligence agencies, working with other countries, have been able to avert a series of planned attacks, including operations in Jordan and the United States during the millennium celebrations.

Some analysts, however, believe those successes enabled bin Laden's resourceful followers to adapt their methods to avoid detection. Bin Laden, for example, stopped using satellite phones after learning that the NSA [National Security Agency] was eavesdropping. This year's trial in New York of the suspected embassy bombers revealed still more about U.S. intelligence methods. In addition, experts speculate that the recent warnings about possible attacks abroad might have been part of a disinformation campaign to mislead U.S. intelligence. Says a former counterterrorism official: "They devised this scheme through the cracks in our procedures."

So while Washington prepared for the worst, the terrorists delivered a low-tech blow. In an age where counterterrorism agencies can sound like Chicken Little—warning constantly about the risks of incoming ballistic missiles or of attacks with chemical and biological weapons—the weapons of choice here were decidedly not sophisticated. Instead of detonating a nuclear device or even a truck bomb, the terrorists transformed the airplanes into missiles, knowing full well the fully fueled jets would ignite infernos on impact. Rather than guns or plastic explosives, the hijackers wielded knives, according to frantic cellphone calls from panicked passengers. "It shows you the vast, almost endless menu of things that people who have this seething hatred of the United States can do," says John Gannon, the former head of the National Intelligence Council.

Airborne Weapon

Airline hijackings were certainly not what officials were expecting. One recent secret Pentagon study, for instance, included vulnerability assessments of dozens of facilities such as reservoirs, airports—and skyscrapers. But the most serious airborne threat was considered to be a small private jet packed with explosives, which would barely have dented the Pentagon and almost certainly would not have collapsed the World Trade Center. A fuel-laden jetliner—not to mention three or four of them—caught even the most careful intelligence analysts by surprise. After all, the last attempted domestic hijacking was a decade ago.

Now the attack is giving new urgency to the debate over how to protect Americans at home, as well as abroad. Perhaps there is no defense against a suicidal pilot in control of an airliner. But security starts in places such as customs posts and airport security lines, both of which are already coming under intense scrutiny. "We have the equivalent of McDonald's handling security at our airports," says counterterrorism expert Johnson, "and it's time to take it seriously as a national security threat." America learned from last week's attack that although the terrorists' grand plan was complex, the tools were simple.

With David E. Kaplan, Edward T. Pound, Richard J. Newman, and Juli Cragg Hilliard

In the following editorial, Fareed Zakaria, an editor for Newsweek *and author of the* New York Times *bestseller* The Future of Freedom, *argues that Al Qaeda's acts of terrorism have been less inspiring to the Islamic world than many people in the United States are led to believe. Bin Laden's philosophy stems from radical Islamic thought, which most of the Muslim community rejects. Zakaria believes that bin Laden's hopes of rousing Muslims to jihad against the United States are perceived by most Muslims as empty solutions offered by a hopeless dreamer.*

Still, as anti-Americanism continues to escalate, terrorist groups remain a major concern to U.S. security. New terrorist groups are forming, and as Al Qaeda morphs, scatters, and recruits, its ambiguous and changing nature makes for a frightening, unknowable, and indestructible foe. —AI

"Bin Laden's Bad Bet"
by Fareed Zakaria
Newsweek, **September 11, 2002**

In one of his legendary moments of brilliance, Sherlock Holmes pointed the attention of the police to the curious behavior of a dog on the night of the murder. The baffled police inspector pointed out that the dog had been silent during the night. "That was the curious incident," explained Holmes. Looking back over the last year, I am reminded of that story because the most important event that has taken place has been a nonevent. Ever since that terrible day in

September 2001, we have all been watching, waiting and listening for the angry voice of Islamic fundamentalism to rip through the Arab and Islamic world. But instead there has been . . . silence. The dog has not barked.

The health of Al Qaeda is a separate matter. Osama bin Laden's organization may be in trouble, but—more likely—it may simply be lying low, plotting in the shadows. In the past it has waited for several years after an operation before staging the next one. Al Qaeda, however, is a band of fanatics, numbering in the thousands. It seeks a much broader following. That, after all, was the point of the attacks of September 11. Bin Laden had hoped that by these spectacular feats of terror he would energize radical movements across the Islamic world. But in the past year it has been difficult to find a major Muslim politician or party or publication that has championed his ideas. In fact, the heated protests over Israel's recent military offensives and American "unilateralism" have obscured the fact that over the past year the fundamentalists have been quiet and in retreat. Radical political Islam—which grew in force and fury ever since the Iranian revolution of 1979—has peaked.

Compare the landscape a decade ago. In Algeria, Islamic fundamentalists, having won an election, were poised to take control of the country. In Turkey, an Islamist political party was gaining ground and would soon also come to power. In Egypt, Hosni Mubarak's regime was terrorized by groups that had effectively shut down the country to foreign tourists. In Pakistan, the mullahs had scared Parliament into enacting blasphemy laws. Only a few years earlier, Iran's Ayatollah Khomeini had issued his fatwa against the novelist Salman

Rushdie, who was still living under armed guard in a secret location. Throughout the Arab world, much of the talk was about political Islam—how to set up an Islamic state, implement Sharia and practice Islamic banking.

Look at these countries now. In Iran, the mullahs still reign but are despised. The governments of Algeria, Egypt, Turkey and (to a lesser extent) Pakistan have all crushed their Islamic groups. Many feared that, as a result, the fundamentalists would become martyrs. In fact, they have had to scramble to survive. In Turkey, the Islamists are now liberals who want to move the country into the European Union. In Algeria, Egypt and elsewhere they are a diminished lot, many of them re-examining their strategy of terror. If the governments brings them into the system, they will go from being mystical figures to local politicians.

Many Islamic groups are lying low; many will still attempt terrorism. But how can a political movement achieve its goals if none dare speak its name? A revolution, especially a transnational one, needs ideologues, pamphlets and party lines to articulate its message to the world. It needs politicians willing to embrace its cause. The Islamic radicals are quiet about their cause for a simple reason. Fewer and fewer people are buying it.

Don't get me wrong. This doesn't mean that people in the Middle East are happy with their regimes or approve of American foreign policy, or that they have come to accept Israel. All these tensions remain strong. But people have stopped looking at Islamic fundamentalism as their salvation. The youth of the 1970s and 1980s, who came from villages into cities and took up Islam as a security blanket, are passing into middle age. The new generation is just as angry, rebellious and bitter. But today's youth grew up in cities and towns, watch Western television shows, buy consumer products and have relatives living in the West. The Taliban holds no allure for them. Most ordinary people have realized that Islamic fundamentalism has no real answers to the problems of the modern world; it has only fantasies. They don't want to replace Western modernity; they want to combine it with Islam.

Alas, none of this will mean the end of our troubles. The Arab world remains a region on the boil. Its demographic, political, economic and social problems are immense and will probably bubble over. Outside the Middle East, in places like Indonesia, the fundamentalists are not yet stale. (Like a supernova whose core has gone dark, radical Islam's light still shines in the periphery.) But you need a compelling ideology to turn frustration into sustained, effective action. After all, Africa has many problems. Yet it is not a mortal threat to the West.

Nor does it mean, alas, the end of terrorism. As they lose political appeal, revolutionary movements often turn more violent. The French scholar Gilles Kepel, who documents the failure of political Islam in his excellent book "Jihad," makes a comparison to communism. It was in the 1960s, after communism had lost any possible appeal to ordinary people—after the revelations about Stalin's brutality, after the invasion of Hungary, as its economic model was decaying—that communist radicals turned to terror. They became members of the Red Brigades, the Stern Gang, the Naxalites, the Shining Path. Having given up on winning the hearts of people, they hoped that violence would intimidate people into fearing them. That is where radical political Islam is today.

For America this means that there is no reason to be gloomy. History is not on the side of the mullahs. If the terrorists are defeated and the fundamentalists are challenged, they will wither. The West must do its part, but above all, moderate Muslims must do theirs. It also means that the cause of reforming the Arab world is not as hopeless as it looks today. We do not confront a region with a powerful alternative to Western ideas, just a place riddled with problems. If these problems are addressed—if its regimes become less repressive, if they reform their economies—the region will, over time, stop breeding terrorists and fanatics. The Japanese once practiced suicide bombing. Now they make computer games.

It might be difficult to see the light from where we are now, still deep in a war against terrorists, with new cells cropping up, new forms of terror multiplying and new methods to spread venomous doctrines. But at his core, the enemy is deadly ill. "This is not the end," as Winston Churchill said in 1942. "It is not even the beginning of the end. But it is the end of the beginning."

With the arrests of high-ranking Al Qaeda members such as Khalid Shaikh Mohammed, U.S. president George W. Bush hit the campaign trail with good news about the war on terror. It was a war that the United States appeared to be winning. The proof was the fact that, since the U.S. invasion of Afghanistan, many criminals

*with ties to Al Qaeda had been locked up in the
Guantánamo Bay, Cuba, detention center. However, as
arrests were made, evidence showed that captured Al
Qaeda members were being replaced by a newer generation
of terrorists. Even as Al Qaeda appeared to be breaking
down, it was spreading itself to all corners of the globe
and creating more, albeit smaller, terrorist groups.*

This New York Times *article reports on how the
seizure of a computer owned by a known Al Qaeda operative has clued investigators in to the inner workings of
the world's most notorious terrorist organization. —AI*

"New Leaders Are Emerging for Al Qaeda"

by David Johnston and David E. Sanger
New York Times, **August 10, 2004**

A new portrait of Al Qaeda's inner workings is emerging
from the cache of information seized last month in Pakistan,
as investigators begin to identify a new generation of operatives who appear to be filling the vacuum created when
leaders were killed or captured, senior intelligence officials
said Monday.

Using computer records, e-mail addresses, and documents
seized after the arrest of Mohammed Naeem Noor Khan last
month in Pakistan, intelligence analysts say they are finding
that Al Qaeda's upper ranks are being filled by lower-ranking
members and more recent recruits.

"They're a little bit of both," one official said, describing
Al Qaeda's new midlevel structure. "Some who have been

around and some who have stepped up. They're reaching for their bench."

While the findings may result in a significant intelligence coup for the Bush administration and its allies in Britain, they also create a far more complex picture of Al Qaeda's status than Mr. Bush presents on the campaign trail. For the past several months, the president has claimed that much of Al Qaeda's leadership has been killed or captured; the new evidence suggests that the organization is regenerating and bringing in new blood.

The new picture emerged from interviews with two officials who have been briefed on some of the details of the intelligence and analytical conclusions drawn from the information on computers seized after Mr. Khan's arrest. But they did not identify the more senior Qaeda leaders, and they said it was not yet clear to what extent Osama bin Laden still exercised control over the organization, either directly or through his chief deputy, Ayman al-Zawahiri.

Officials say they still do not have a clear picture of the midlevel structure that exists between Mr. Khan, who appeared to be responsible for communications but not operations, and the upper echelons of Al Qaeda.

The new evidence suggests that Al Qaeda has retained some elements of its previous centralized command and communications structure, using computer experts like Mr. Khan to relay encrypted messages and directions from leaders to subordinates in countries like Britain, Turkey and Nigeria.

In the past, officials had a different view of Al Qaeda. After the American-led war in Afghanistan, most American counterterrorism analysts believed that the group had been dispersed and had been trying to re-form in a loosely affiliated collection of extremist groups.

It appears that Al Qaeda is more resilient than was previously understood and has sought to find replacements for operational commanders like Khalid Shaikh Mohammed, Abu Zubaydah and Walid Muhammad Salih bin Attash, known as Khallad, all of whom have been captured.

Mr. bin Laden and Mr. Zawahiri are believed to be in hiding in the region along the border between Afghanistan and Pakistan. In July, when American officials announced that Al Qaeda intended to strike inside the United States this year, they said that they believed Mr. bin Laden was directing the threats.

The names of senior members of the terror network were not discussed by the intelligence officials, in part, they said, to avoid compromising efforts to kill or capture them. "They are in Pakistan or the region," said one official, who also said that the Pakistani government was being "quite helpful" in helping identify them. That is a significant change from last year, but the attitude of Pakistan's president, Gen. Pervez Musharraf, appeared to change after he survived two assassination attempts that are now believed to have been aided by Qaeda sympathizers. "That focused his mind on the issue," one American said.

The Khan computer files also led to the arrest of 11 Qaeda followers last week in Britain. They are described by officials as young, alienated Arab men with extreme anti-American views, much like many of Mr. bin Laden's foot soldiers and many of the 19 men who took part in the attacks of Sept. 11, 2001.

One key figure among the men arrested in Britain is Abu Issa al-Hindi, who is believed to have supervised the surveillance of financial institutions in New York, New Jersey, and Washington. He appears to represent what authorities said was a different kind of Qaeda recruit, a convert to Islam who did not appear to have been trained in Mr. bin Laden's Afghanistan camps.

The arrest of Mr. Khan continued to be debated on Monday in the capital. A Democratic senator, Charles E. Schumer of New York, asked the White House to explain how the identity of the communications expert arrested in Pakistan last month became publicly known.

Mr. Schumer said in a letter to Condoleezza Rice, the national security adviser, that the disclosure of Mr. Khan's capture may have complicated efforts to combat terror.

The apprehension of Mr. Khan led authorities in Pakistan to computers that provided a wealth of information about Al Qaeda operations, including the surveillance of the financial institutions. It remains unclear whether he was cooperating with Pakistani intelligence at the time of his arrest or had previously provided Islamabad with information about Al Qaeda.

"I believe that openness in government is generally the best policy," Mr. Schumer wrote. "But the important exception should be anything that compromises national security. The statements of the British and Pakistani officials indicate that such a compromise may have occurred."

There have been reports of Pakistani officials complaining that public statements in the United States about Mr. Khan's arrest gave his Qaeda contacts notice that they may be under surveillance.

Mr. bin Laden's precise role in the leadership of his organization remains murky. After the Sept. 11 attacks he did not appear to take an active leadership role in formulating a specific plan, as he had in the Sept. 11 plot, administration officials have said. At times he has appeared to be struggling to maintain his primacy as the leader of the network through messages exhorting his followers to carry out operations against American targets.

But in recent months, there has been evidence leading some analysts to conclude that Mr. bin Laden may have been able to maintain greater control over planning for attacks.

CHAPTER TWO

PEOPLE, PLACES, AND ENVIRONMENTS: WHO AND WHERE IS AL QAEDA?

In 1996, Osama bin Laden left Sudan for Afghanistan where he befriended Mullah Mohammed Omar, the head of the Taliban, and subsequently forged an alliance with him. It was not the first time bin Laden had been involved in Afghanistan's military and political plights. During the Soviet occupation, bin Laden had funded and fought alongside the mujahideen in what is considered one of the longest and most important jihads of modern history. This time bin Laden was supporting Taliban efforts to unite the country under one leadership. In return, bin Laden was able to use the Taliban-controlled Afghanistan as a base of operations for Al Qaeda.

The following account of the Taliban's rise to power and the lawless, troubled state of Afghanistan comes from the book The Age of Sacred Terror, *by Daniel Benjamin and Steven Simon. Both authors served as National Security Council directors for counterterrorism under the Clinton administration. —AI*

From *The Age of Sacred Terror*
by Daniel Benjamin and Steven Simon
2002

A core tenet of al-Qaeda's strategy is that radical Islamists must gain control of a nation, from which they can then expand the area controlled by believers. Holding a state, in their view, is the prelude to knocking over the dominoes of the world's secular Muslim regimes. "Armies achieve victory only when the infantry takes hold of land," Ayman al-Zawahiri has written. "Likewise, the mujahid Islamic movement will not triumph against the world coalition unless it possesses a fundamentalist base in the heart of the Islamic world." The craving for territory is one reason why al-Qaeda carries out its own terrorist attacks and supports so many national insurgencies. Winning a country will be no easy task, but the stakes are enormous, for only thus can the "Muslim nation reinstate its fallen caliphate and regain its lost glory." Al-Zawahiri cites history as proof: not until Muslim forces in the twelfth century united Syria and Egypt could Saladin—a revered figure among jihadists—defeat the Crusaders at the battle of Hattin in 1187 and retake Jerusalem. "Only then did the cycle of history turn."

Bin Laden and his followers had hoped that this germinal state would be Sudan. The country's leaders may have entertained the same thought, but they ultimately did not share the Saudi's vision of how to make that happen. Bin Laden returned to Afghanistan in May 1996, a disappointed man. If there was a hell on earth, this was it. After seventeen years of war, the country was utterly destroyed—as failed as a state could be.

Nearly one and a half million people were dead, and at least two and a half million more were in exile. Afghanistan's irrigation systems were mined, its livestock herds had shrunk, and much farmland and pasture was unusable because it had been sown with hundreds of thousands of land mines. A bare subsistence was all most people could hope for. Average life expectancy stood at a medieval forty-six years; the infant mortality rate, 147 per 1,000 births, was more than twenty-five times that in the United States. Public order had vanished. Warring armies ranged across the countryside, and gunmen pillaged, raped, and killed with abandon.

One important thing had changed: after years of seesawing battles between rival factions of mujahidin, a new force had emerged determined to end the internecine warfare. The Taliban, literally "the students," was born in 1994. There is no shortage of founding myths about the group, but the one most often cited is set in Kandahar province: two teenage girls had been kidnapped and repeatedly raped by followers of an area warlord. An outraged village cleric, Mullah Mohammed Omar, gathered together thirty students and attacked the camp where the girls were being held. They freed the captives and hanged the group's commander from the barrel of a tank.

Soon, this small band was raiding the camps of powerful warlords, building stocks of weapons and ammunition, and attracting more students. It drew support from the religiously oriented political parties in Pakistan, which are dominated by Deobandi Muslims, who run many of the madrassas or religious schools, in the Afghan refugee camps and elsewhere. After a series of daring Taliban successes, the Pakistani government began backing the new force as well. Islamabad wanted to break the deadlock among the warring factions that made Afghanistan ungovernable, blocked trade with Central Asia, and kept refugees from going home. The regime also glimpsed in the Taliban the possibility of breathing life into a creature that could aid its own interests.

Within Afghanistan, the Taliban enjoyed a growing popularity. It provided something that ordinary Afghans longed for: a modicum of order. Chaos had reigned for so many years that people had become accustomed to being treated like the chattel of the warlords, or worse. The Taliban vanquished many marauding bands and disarmed trouble-makers.

But stability came at a price: the Taliban enforced an extreme brand of Islamic practice that had evolved in Afghan villages and refugee camps, a fusion between the radical Wahhabism taught by Saudi missionaries and the comparably hardline Deobandi belief of the Pakistani madrassas, themselves an offshoot of the Wahhabism that had taken root in South Asia in the nineteenth century. Amputations and stonings became common punishments for crimes; due process had little role in the "legal" system. One Taliban specialty was to crush those who committed certain infractions—homosexuality is one example—by knocking walls over onto them. Another effect of the rise of the Taliban was that from one day to the next, women were forced out of their jobs, forbidden to appear alone in public, and compelled to wear the head-to-toe burqa. But crime rates fell, and the restoration of some semblance of personal safety in a country that had known none in recent memory, as well as the evident incorruptibility of the Taliban, attracted recruits in droves. Young men and boys flocked

from madrassas in Afghanistan and the refugee camps of
Pakistan.

After the Taliban's success in capturing Kandahar,
Afghanistan's second largest city, at the end of 1994, the
group acquired an aura of invincibility. There were occasional
setbacks, but with the backing of Pakistan and Saudi Arabia,
Taliban fighters—undisciplined but unrelenting—subdued one
province after another. In September 1996 they laid siege to
Kabul, then ruled by the government of Burhannudin Rabbani
and his military commander, Ahmad Shah Massoud. Later that
month, when the Taliban broke through, the first thing its soldiers did was hunt down Najibullah, the Afghan communist
who had been in power until 1992. For four years, since his
fall from power, the former ruler had been taking refuge in a
UN compound, whose sanctuary the Rabbani government
respected. The Taliban was no observer of such diplomatic
niceties: its gunmen broke into the compound, beat and cas-
trated Najibullah, dragged him behind a jeep, shot him, and
strung him up from a traffic post, along with his brother.
Pictures of the bloodstreaked and bloated bodies appeared
throughout the world.

. . . Around the world, many believers, including some
Islamists in Egypt and Saudi Arabia, viewed the Taliban with
distaste as primitive, unschooled, and unruly. Even the mullahs of the Pakistani madrassas, who had educated many of
the Taliban leaders, would speak of them as well-meaning but
occasionally excessive in their zeal. But if bin Laden had any
such reservations about his new hosts, he never voiced them.
He seems to have settled without hesitation into his life as an
honored guest of the state.

We know little about the ties between him and the Taliban in this period. According to a Pakistani news story that appeared after the first meeting of bin Laden and Mullah Omar, in March 1997, the Afghan leader issued a statement saying that the United States should leave Saudi Arabia "because they risked losing the sympathy of Muslims." It is interesting that the apparent subject of their discussion was bin Laden's issue, not Omar's. And, in fact, al-Qaeda seems to have been surprised that a good relationship, was established so quickly with the Afghan regime.

. . . But if Omar was welcoming from the outset, he was not typical of his countrymen. As a group, the Arab Afghans, several thousands of whom were still in the country and hundreds more came back with bin Laden, were little liked by the populace, which considered them outsiders and dangerous fanatics. The Taliban was less hostile—much of its funding came from Wahhabi sources in the Persian Gulf—but even so, al-Qaeda devoted considerable energy and money to endearing itself to its new hosts as part of an effort to bend Afghanistan to its own purposes.

The Taliban had numerous needs and one overriding priority: complete the military conquest of Afghanistan. It had rolled over of the country's provinces in the mid-1990s only to find itself in a stalemate with the Northern Alliance forces led by Ahmad Shah Massoud, the former military commander of the government the Taliban toppled. Each year, when winter receded, the two sides would battle each other across northern Afghanistan. But the Taliban could not inflict a decisive defeat on Massoud, a superb general who always managed to hold on to about 15 percent of the country and then, at the end of each fighting season, withdraw to his stronghold in the remote Panjshir Valley. The Taliban received the bulk of its supplies from Pakistan. But bin Laden ingratiated himself with the movement's corps commanders by providing them with additional weaponry and, more important, detachments of fighters.

Much had changed over the many years of combat. The earlier generations of fearless Afghan warriors had faded into memory, and for all their spirit, the Taliban lacked military know-how. The Arab Afghans were now combat hardened, and the Taliban commanders were grateful for their services. Bin Laden's largesse in this regard was so great that high-ranking Taliban officers constituted a hard core of support for him.

His generosity did not stop with the military. He provided Taliban leaders with infusions of much-needed cash, and he imported fleets of Toyota Land Cruisers, the official vehicle of jihad, which he distributed to Taliban worthies. Eventually, his generosity gained him a measure of acceptance from ordinary Afghans. During a time when foreign aid workers were increasingly reluctant to work in Afghanistan because of the restrictions put upon them by the Taliban, bin Laden became a critical source of support, funding hospitals and doling out food.

In 2001, Jason Burke, a British reporter for the Observer, *was granted a tour of Khaldan camp in Afghanistan, a terrorism school that had been run by Osama bin Laden. The camp had been deserted since September 11, but the evidence left behind proved a*

major aid to the U.S. war on terror. The camp provided especially useful intelligence on Al Qaeda, including the extent of its operations, names of key leaders, and insight into the group's chain of command. The camp, as Burke discovers, was not merely a training facility, but also served as a laboratory for the creation of new terrorist operations.

Inspecting the camp gave Burke a harrowing glimpse at the integral role these schools played in spreading bin Laden's ideologies and terrorist network. Bin Laden was believed to have come to the camps and hand-picked students for certain duties in his terrorist plots. The Commission on Terrorism estimates that approximately 20,000 people studied at bin Laden's camps throughout Afghanistan. —AI

"Hidden Letters Reveal Dark Secrets of School for Terror"
by Jason Burke
Observer, November 25, 2001

Abu Said al-Kurdi is gone. So are his students. And so are their guns and their bombs and their chemical warfare kits. All that remains of the training camp that was Abu Said's home for the last five years are four blocks of drab grey bungalows, an empty library and, in a corner where a bank of computers once stood, a small stack of documents.

They are all that reveals this rambling compound in the outskirts of the dusty eastern Afghan city of Khowst as perhaps the most significant terrorist training centre in the world.

For the stack of papers includes letters addressed to "Khaldan Camp"—known to law enforcement agencies worldwide as Osama bin Laden's "university of terror." Not only do the letters give an amazing insight into the lives and minds of the men who lived and trained in Khaldan camp but they also reveal startling new evidence about a string of terrorist atrocities that law enforcement officials have been trying for years to pin on the Saudi-born terrorist mastermind.

They reveal the extent of his international network, link him directly to the bombing of the American embassies in East Africa three years ago and to the murderous kidnapping in Yemen in 1999, and prove that his men were interested in developing chemical weapons.

Khaldan camp is where, according to their own confessions, the men who bombed the East African embassies were handpicked by bin Laden's lieutenants. At least two of the 11 September hijackers, possibly including Mohamed Atta, the group's leader, are also believed by the FBI to have trained there and in further camps around Khowst.

This is the dark heart of Osama bin Laden's terrorist network. For half a decade no Westerner has been to Khowst, let alone to the al-Qaeda camps, safe houses, mosques, residence halls and workshops that litter the city and the surrounding areas.

When they fled, the Arabs gutted their former bases in the city. They are not far away—most have moved out to their military camp at Jawran, just 10 miles away. But they have left enough clues behind them to give an idea of what they were doing. Not far from Khaldan camp—under one of the Arab safe houses—a cellar full of barrels of chemicals has been found. Its entrance is surrounded by dead birds.

The Observer was also able to see how Khowst, a dusty town in eastern Afghanistan set on a rocky plain ringed by baked and blasted mountains, had become the virtual fiefdom of bin Laden. The city, site of vicious battles against the Soviet occupiers in the eighties, was captured by the Taliban who took control in 1996. They virtually ceded the city to their Arab extremist allies.

Though the Taliban retained a governor and the semblance of an administration Khowst effectively fell under the control of bin Laden and his group. A huge, half-built mosque, constructed over the last five years with donations from al-Qaeda supporters in the Gulf, now dominates the city's skyline. Nearby is a large hospital built by the Arabs in the last three years for those injured in the battles alongside their Taliban allies. Bin Laden has a house in the city from where he has issued statements and given interviews. Hundreds of recruits to al-Qaeda were living in Khowst, many with their families, at any one time. Almost all the thousands of Islamic extremist volunteers who have been trained in Afghanistan or fought with the Taliban at any stage since bin Laden arrived back in the country in 1996 have been through the city. It has long been considered the base of the Arab "international brigade" operating in Afghanistan.

But when Kabul fell to the opposition 12 days ago Khowst became impossible to defend. The Taliban pulled back to their southern stronghold of Kandahar. Many of the al-Qaeda fighters fled across the border to Pakistan two hours' drive away, allowing a local warlord, Bacha Khan Zardan, to take control.

To prove his hold on the city and to demonstrate that he had expelled the Arabs, he agreed last week to take *The Observer* to the town.

The journey took two days. Bacha Khan's claims of "complete security" in the areas he controlled proved to be over-confident. Our heavily armed convoy travelled by remote mountain roads through tribal territory loyal to the warlord to avoid political enemies and bandits on the main highways.

We were told to dress in local clothing and to hide beneath a blanket when the convoy passed through villages. Only days before our arrival American jets had destroyed a mosque and religious college on the edge of the town, killing around 100 al-Qaeda men and Taliban soldiers. As our convoy sped past the rubble—still being picked through by bin Laden sympathisers—our guards readied their weapons. But the city itself was quiet and there was no one in Khaldan camp but Bacha Khan's own soldiers.

The most obvious evidence of al-Qaeda's interest were the English-language manuals left in a bundle in the former library. Many of the hundreds of pages of photocopied pages appear to have come from the infamous "terrorist's cookbook" circulated by far-right extremists in America and elsewhere.

One 41-page document entitled "Assorted Nasties" is a "how to" guide to chemical weapons. It describes itself as covering "a myriad of lethal materials, ranging from those which may be cooked up (literally) in the kitchen, to those requiring a sophisticated lab set-up. Most are not beyond the range of anyone familiar with proper laboratory technique."

The book goes on to describe how to make a variety of chemical weapons ranging from mustard gas to sarin and explains a variety of different delivery mechanisms. Other manuals cover favoured bomb designs of Middle Eastern terrorists, car bombs and explosives manufacture. Several books in Arabic give details of similar topics. Most interesting are the personal letters that *The Observer* found at the site. Several mention bin Laden by name. One, written to Abu Said by another senior trainer from the Yemen called Abu Ziad, refers to orders received from bin Laden himself. "I have sat and spoken to Sheikh Osama . . . and he has made arrangements for me to travel to Eritrea. I am going to stay there for a month and a half, then I am going to travel, and then I am praying to God that I will be martyred," it says.

Though the letter is undated, most of those found in a packet with it are from April and May of 1998. The East African embassy bombings took place in August. The identities of the suicide bombers are still unclear, though it is known that many of the terrorist team that carried out the attack travelled through the Yemen.

Several letters also refer to the creation of a Yemeni terrorist cell on bin Laden's orders. In an astonishing breach of security, the number of a PO box in Sanaa, the Yemeni capital, is given. There are mentions of the man who was to lead the group who kidnapped and killed British tourists in the Yemen in December 1999. That attack has never previously been directly linked to bin Laden.

One large batch of letters are "thank you" notes to Abu Said from former students. Some talk about "further training" at other camps on the outskirts of Khowst, such as the infamous "al-Farooq" base where advanced instruction was given to those recruits picked out by their tutors.

According to the FBI and a Gulf intelligence agency's secret dossier obtained by *The Observer* in September, two of the terrorists who attacked the World Trade Centre were sent to al-Farooq after passing through Khaldan camp.

The letters give suggestions for improvements to the course. Most criticisms are concerned with tactics. Many ask for a greater emphasis on urban guerrilla warfare. "All the tyrants who are our enemies are in cities. We must learn how to strike them there," says one.

This tallies with intelligence reports that Khaldan camp was a general training camp providing instruction in basic infantry tactics. More specialised skills were taught elsewhere. An exercise book found at the camp by *The Observer* is full of information about small arms, grenades, ambushes, and other tactical skills. From their letters the recruits seem eager to progress to assassinations and more advanced operations.

There are some human touches. Many talk of the "self-discipline" and "inner strength" they have found. One student writes that the recruits did not mix well, with those from the same nations sticking together. Names in the letters, which are often written in poor Arabic, reveal that students came from Tajikistan, Saudi Arabia, the Yemen, Bosnia, Turkistan, Pakistan, Algeria, Iraq, and Egypt. One letter complains that Abu Said was "very serious all the time" and never joked or laughed with the students.

One former student thanks Said. "I am grateful for being taught how faith and good tactics can overcome an enemy that is physically bigger and stronger," he wrote.

Since the invasion of Afghanistan, the United States has
taken several of Al Qaeda's leaders into custody. Perhaps
the most important capture to date was that of Khalid
Shaikh Mohammed, a master propagandist for the group
and a planner of the September 11, 2001, attacks. His
arrest seriously maimed Al Qaeda operations. Although
the capture of so many key players may sound like good
news, David Kaplan and Kevin Whitelaw argue in the
November 1, 2004, U.S. News and World Report *that*
the world is far from safe from Al Qaeda operations.
They paint a portrait of a new Al Qaeda, a farther-
reaching and more ambiguous organization, for which
bin Laden is an inspiration rather than a leader.

Kaplan and Whitelaw's article suggests that Al
Qaeda is an even larger threat than it once was now that
offshoots have been surfacing all over the globe. Because
there is no centralization, they argue, there is no clearly
defined target. The article brings to light a terrifying
quandary: is the U.S. war on terror only inciting more
terrorist organizations around the world? —AI

"Terror's New Soldiers"
by David E. Kaplan and Kevin Whitelaw
U.S. News and World Report, November 1, 2004

He was known simply as "Electronic." Nabbed last week in
Pakistan holding a Canadian passport, Abdul Rahman, allegedly
an Arab communications expert for al Qaeda, is among the latest of thousands of suspects seized since 9/11. But now a new
generation of militants is emerging. As with so much in the war
on terrorism, it's hard to tell if it is being won or lost.

Terrorism concerns are driving much of the debate in the presidential campaign, which has unfolded amid a stream of terrorism alerts at home and attacks abroad. Yet many Americans still have only a limited understanding of who, exactly, the enemy is and whether the nation is safer. In his standard stump speeches, President Bush makes his case: "Because we acted, a free Afghanistan is fighting terror; Pakistan is capturing terrorist leaders; Saudi Arabia is making arrests; Libya is dismantling its weapons programs; the Army of a free Iraq is fighting for freedom; and more than three quarters of al Qaeda have been brought to justice."

But take that final statistic: The three-quarters figure refers only to al Qaeda's top leadership before September 11. This included some of al Qaeda's most capable operatives, including 9/11 mastermind Khalid Shaikh Mohammed, who are now in custody. But Osama bin Laden and his deputy, Ayman al-Zawahiri, remain at large. And many leadership gaps have been filled by other operatives, albeit men less experienced.

"Petri Dish"

More worrisome, the nature of the enemy is changing. The al Qaeda of 9/11 is gone. Once a sprawling, multimillion-dollar operation with its own training camps, businesses, and even guesthouses, al Qaeda lost much of its infrastructure in the 2001 invasion of Afghanistan and later crackdowns. In its place has emerged a more elusive foe, a loosely affiliated network linked together by local militants, the Internet, and a shared ideology of radical Sunni Islam. "Al Qaeda has transformed from a group," says terrorism consultant Rohan Gunaratna, "into a movement."

Al Qaeda was always a sum of many parts, relying on local groups from Indonesia to Uzbekistan. But bin Laden has spread his ideology successfully enough that new, homegrown groups are emerging. Local jihadists in Spain and Turkey conducted some of the past year's deadliest bombings—and few were veterans of al Qaeda's camps. "The next battle will be over the localized groups that are springing up," says Cofer Black, the State Department's counterterrorism chief. "They are vulnerable to radical thought." One intelligence analyst sees conditions in many Muslim communities—poverty, inequality, and anger over the Israeli-Palestinian crisis—as a "petri dish for jihadists." He warns, "We're cranking out more and more jihadists, and they're getting smarter."

And then there's the Iraq war. No issue more sharply divides the two presidential candidates, who disagree about whether the Iraq invasion was even part of the war on terrorism. Bush argues that the war is key to transforming the region and that fighting terrorists there has kept them away from America. But experts on radical Islam broadly agree that at least the short-term effects aren't good. Officials who monitor what one analyst calls "the internal conversations in Islam"—in the media and the mosques—report alarming levels of anti-Americanism. "Our actions have gotten the fundamentalists more energized than anybody in the last century," says Milt Bearden, who ran CIA operations in Afghanistan and Pakistan during the 1980s. "They believe Bush has declared war on Islam."

Terrorists' Dentists

All of which makes it much harder to gauge success. Intelligence officials frequently refer to Defense Secretary

Donald Rumsfeld's memo last year, in which he asked: "Are we capturing, killing or deterring and dissuading more terrorists every day than the madrassas and the radical clerics are recruiting, training and deploying against us?" Data are hard to come by. A report issued by the British-based International Institute for Strategic Studies last week estimates that at least 20,000 jihadists were trained in al Qaeda's Afghan camps since 1996 but that only some 2,000 rank-and-file members have been captured or killed.

This much is clear—the war is getting harder to fight. Despite technological advantages and unprecedented global cooperation, U.S. intelligence agencies are not well suited to tracking scattered bands of militants. "As it morphs from an organization to a movement, how do you delineate who is related and who is affiliated—who is a terrorist and who is a cousin?" says a senior U.S. intelligence official. "Even terrorists have dentists."

More broadly, many observers worry that the nation has not fully mobilized to counter the threat. "There is a tremendous reluctance on the part of those who have been through the Cold War to admit that another one is aborning," says a senior U.S. official. The solutions range from addressing some of the vast inequities to an overhaul of America's public-outreach efforts. "We're not going to get this right," warns James Pavitt, who retired last summer after running the CIA's Clandestine Service, "if we don't deal with the root causes—economic, social, and cultural."

With Aamir Latif, in Pakistan

*In this editorial printed in the aftermath of September
11, 2001, author and military historian Caleb Carr
argues that U.S. generalizations and denunciations of
terrorists have hindered the investigation and attempts
to capture them. Carr argues that U.S. authorities have
been viewing Al Qaeda terrorists as mentally unstable
suicide bombers instead of as soldiers with a style of
methodical warfare, however different it is from the U.S.
code of war etiquette.*

*This opinion piece attempts to reason with the post–
September 11, 2001, fury that pervaded the American
psyche. Because the attacks on the World Trade Center and
the Pentagon were so incomprehensible to people, many
outraged Americans, including high-ranking members of
the U.S. government, resorted to sweeping generalizations
of the nature of an enemy that would attack in such a
way. To combat an enemy by brushing off his methods of
warfare as fanatical and insane, Carr argues, is to dan-
gerously underestimate the threat of such an enemy. —AI*

"The Art of Knowing the Enemy"
by Caleb Carr
New York Times, December 21, 2001

Both the Justice Department and the American intelligence
community have proved as incapable of assembling useful psychological profiles of Islamic terrorists since Sept. 11 as they
were of identifying such people in the months leading up to
the attacks.

The first duty of any law enforcement or military officer
is to "know your enemy." Yet President Bush continues to

refer to Osama bin Laden and his associates, like those on the videotape of Mr. bin Laden released last week, merely as "evil people"—the sort of simplistic moral denunciation that only makes the behavior of terrorists more incomprehensible by ascribing to them vague and inaccurate motives. The Justice Department continues to view Mr. bin Laden's terrorist followers essentially as criminals and continues to employ tactics that would seem of more use against smugglers, drug dealers or racketeers than against religious soldiers. Attorney General John Ashcroft's roundup of hundreds of supposedly suspicious aliens, a tactic worthy of a small-town police department, is revealing of a particularly archaic approach to suspect profiling.

We can do better—indeed, the military, under Donald Rumsfeld's leadership, has moved past the "evil people" paradigm by recognizing that terrorism is (as its practitioners have always insisted) a form of warfare, and that terrorists themselves, whether evil or not, are a variety of soldier.

In the terrorists' own minds, theirs is a fight inspired by faith, and like most religious warriors throughout history, they consider uniforms, codes of conduct, and national loyalties irrelevant. In the name of their lofty cause they have organized into highly disciplined units, trained hard with up-to-date weapons, assembled effective intelligence and counterintelligence services, and learned to use sophisticated information technology. We may resent the idea of according such shadowy but deadly people the same status as our own servicemen and women—but they are an army nonetheless, and it has been the willingness of the Rumsfeld regime at the Pentagon to engage them as such that has led to the successes achieved in Afghanistan.

At home, law-enforcement officials refer to Mohamed Atta, suspected as the ringleader of the Sept. 11 hijackers, as a criminal mastermind rather than as a military lieutenant dutifully following orders. The men he led are called suicide attackers, as if they were puppets afflicted with some sort of self-destructive psychosis rather than troops employing what is an extreme but by no means unusual military tactic: sacrificing their own handful of lives to achieve an overall objective deemed vital to their cause.

This basic error in profiling—treating terrorists as criminals rather than as soldiers—is the source from which other errors have sprung and continue to flow. What sane man, our officials have reasoned, abandons a loving family to engage in a suicidal crime? So the attackers must be insane. Yet would those same American officials and analysts make similar pronouncements about our own special forces troops who have died in high-risk operations? The willingness to sacrifice one's own life is not, in the context of military psychology, a foolproof gauge of mental imbalance. It can just as often—perhaps far more often—be evidence of a deep commitment.

Our lack of understanding of these men has even colored our interpretation of the bin Laden videotape. Even among anti–bin Laden Muslim commentators, there has been little if any suggestion that his occasional chuckling on the tape is intended as mockery of the Qaeda members who died in the attacks, as American officials characterized it. Rather, he is seen as expressing awe at the extent of their discipline and the damage they inflicted—just as Americans might quietly and admiringly chuckle at the amazing bravery and effectiveness of their own dead soldiers.

The mistaken ideas that Mr. bin Laden is scoffing at his followers and that the average Islamic terrorist is an unbalanced, suicidal misfit are more than just useless: this sort of profiling actively hampers the kind of genuine understanding that will help American citizens engage in constructive discrimination between those few Muslims who may be dangerous and the far greater number who have been placed under the pall of suspicion simply by virtue of their names, their nationalities and their religion.

As events of the last century in places ranging from Germany to the Soviet Union to Cambodia should have taught us, an army of aggrieved but otherwise unremarkable people can place itself at the service of an utterly deluded leader, commit horrific atrocities in that leader's name and yet still remain, in each of its soldiers' minds, an honorable force defending its home and its values.

To fight terrorism, we need a far more accurate understanding of Osama bin Laden's appeal, as well as of the types of personalities that are most strongly affected by his call to arms, than the administration has offered. The government needs to formulate more detailed psychological profiles of this particular enemy. We should then make public these profiles so that they can be used to help our law enforcement officers get on with the business of thwarting terrorist attacks without resorting to useless exercises that target masses of innocent people. We have to be as progressive about our domestic defense as we have been in the use of our armed forces abroad.

In the following article, Peter David of the Economist *provides a short history of religious fundamentalism in the Muslim world. At the center of the discussion is Sayyid Qutb, a Muslim intellectual who encouraged a radical form of Islam until he was executed in 1966. According to the author, Qutb's beliefs were similar to the beliefs of members of Al Qaeda, including Osama bin Laden.*

A common thread in Qutb's writing was his denunciation of Western values, specifically those of the United States. These ideas have become popular throughout Muslim society, and scholars like Qutb are at least partly responsible for these trends.

Today, Western scholars and politicians are trying to better understand the origins of the conflict between the Muslim world and the non-Muslim world. According to the author, at the heart of the conflict is Islam, a religion that influences politics and culture in Muslim society in ways more complex than the way Christianity influences Western society. —AI

"In the Name of Islam"
by Peter David
Economist, **September 13, 2003**

"The next war, they say." That was the headline printed at the top of this page the last time *The Economist* published a survey of Islam, in August 1994. We concluded that conflict between Islam and the West was by no means impossible. But the writer of our survey was not convinced that it was inevitable. Another possibility was that the anger and disillusionment that seemed to be sweeping through the world of Islam in the 1990s might turn in a more benign direction. Was it not similar to the disillusionment that began to sweep through Christendom in the 16th century, which led via the Reformation to the development of modern democracy?

To some, the falling of the twin towers two years ago this week offers dramatic evidence that the bleaker forecasts of the 1990s were right. What was this attack if not the start of a new war between the civilisations? Many Muslims do not like the label "Islamic terrorism" attached to the mass murders perpetrated by Osama bin Laden and his al-Qaeda organisation. Islam, they say, is a religion of peace, a peace, which has no more connection to the terrorism of Mr. bin Laden than Christianity had to the 1970s terrorism of, say, the Baader-Meinhof gang in Germany or the Red Brigades in Italy. Just call it terrorism, they say: keep Islam out of it.

That is not quite possible. When people are trying to kill you, especially when they are good at it, it is prudent to listen to the reasons they give. And Mr. bin Laden launched his "war" explicitly in Islam's name. Indeed, three years before the twin towers, he went to the trouble of issuing a lengthy "Declaration of the World Islamic Front for Jihad against the Jews and the Crusaders," stating that "to kill Americans and their allies, both civil and military, is the individual duty of every Muslim who is able, until the Aqsa mosque [in Jerusalem] and the Haram mosque [in Mecca] are freed from their grip, and until their armies, shattered and broken-winged, depart from all the lands of Islam."

It may be objected that any bunch of psychopaths bent on mayhem is free to say whatever it likes about its motives.

Just because al-Qaeda's people kill in the name of Islam does not mean that conflict with the West is an essential part of the faith. A Marxist terrorist may say that he is killing for the sake of the working class, and that he possesses a whole body of theory to justify this activity, and that this theory is subscribed to by many people. Does that mean that it is somehow in the essence of the working class to wage war on capitalism? No. But it does suggest that societies trying to deal with Marxist terrorism need to look at Marxist ideas, and gauge the extent to which they are believed.

By the same token, the problem for those who want to believe that Islam has nothing to do with Islamic terrorism is not only that the terrorists themselves say otherwise. It is also the existence of a whole body of theory that is called upon to justify this activity, and which has zealous adherents. Admittedly, much of this theory is modern, as political as it is religious, with origins in the late 20th century. It is described variously as "fundamentalism," "Islamism," or "political Islam" (though these terms and definitions will need closer inspection later). But some of it also has, or claims to have, connections with some of the fundamental ideas and practices of the religion itself.

Allah or Ignorance

A good place to start to understand the theory is with the ideas of Sayyid Qutb, a literary critic in the 1930s and 1940s and later an activist in Egypt's Muslim Brotherhood before being executed in 1966. In the late 1940s, Qutb spent two years living in America, an experience he hated and which appears to have turned him against what most people in the

West would call modernity but which he saw as something much worse.

On returning to Egypt, Qutb wrote a series of books, many from prison, denouncing jahiliyya (ignorance), a state of affairs he categorised as the domination of man over man, or rather subservience to man rather than to Allah. Such a state of affairs, he said, had existed in the past, existed in the present and threatened to continue in the future. It was the sworn enemy of Islam. "In any time and place human beings face that clear-cut choice: either to observe the law of Allah in its entirety, or to apply laws laid down by man of one sort or another. That is the choice: Islam or jahiliyya. Modern-style jahiliyya in the industrialised societies of Europe and America is essentially similar to the old-time jahiliyya in pagan and nomadic Arabia. For in both systems, man is under the dominion of man rather than Allah."

Qutb was not the first Muslim intellectual to look at the world this way. He was influenced by a contemporary, Maulana Maudoodi in India, who was also repelled by modernity and saw it as barbarism. Both men drew on earlier episodes and thinkers. One such was a medieval theologian, Taqi al-Din ibn Taymiyya, a sort of Muslim Luther who in reaction to the Mongol onslaught of the 13th century preached a return to the essentials of the faith, which the ulema (clerics) of the time had forsaken. Another, in the 18th century, was Muhammad ibn Abd al-Wahhab, who advocated purging Islam of modern accretions and relying strictly on the Koran and hadith (the record of the prophet's words and deeds). But it is Qutb's story that offers the more interesting insight into the way Islamic terrorists think today.

One reason is that Qutb is a link with the present. The Muslim Brothers continue to operate in Egypt and elsewhere. Mr. bin Laden and his deputy, Ayman al-Zawahiri, are former Brothers. More than this, the forces that Qutb believed to be undermining Islam in the 1950s and 1960s—capitalism, individualism, promiscuity, decadence—are still seen as potent threats (more potent, with "globalisation") by Muslims today.

Qutb lost faith in the pan-Arab nationalism that was the prevailing ideology of the Arab world in his own time. In a letter from prison he said that the homeland a Muslim should cherish was not a piece of land but the whole Dar al-Islam (Abode of Islam). Any land that hampered the practice of Islam or failed to apply sharia law "becomes ipso facto part of Dar al-Harb (the Abode of War). It should be combated even if one's own kith and kin, national group, capital and commerce are to be found there."

A straight line connects Qutb's letter from prison to the ideas of Mr. bin Laden and his followers in al-Qaeda. Like Qutb, al-Qaeda's followers perceive Islam to be under a double attack: not just military attack from a hostile West (in Iraq, Palestine, Chechnya and so forth) but also from within, where western values spread by impious regimes are undermining what it means to be a Muslim. This double attack, in the al-Qaeda world view, is to be resisted by jihad in both of the two meanings this notion has in Islam: personal striving for a more perfect submission to the faith, and armed struggle against Islam's enemies. These enemies include both the far enemy (America, Israel) and the near enemy (the impious or even apostate regimes of the Muslim world). For Mr. bin Laden, the Saudi regime is now as much his enemy as is the United States.

How representative are such views? Around one in four of the people in the world are Muslims. Only a small fraction of these 1.5 billion Muslims will have heard of, let alone subscribe to, the ideas of theorists such as Qutb. No more than a few thousand people are involved in the violent activities of al-Qaeda and like-minded jihadi organisations. After September 11th, moreover, Muslim clerics and intellectuals joined ordinary Muslims throughout the world in denouncing the atrocity al-Qaeda had perpetrated in their name. By no means all of these were "moderates." One was Sheikh Fadlallah, the Beirut-based ayatollah often described as the spiritual guide of Hizbullah, the Iranian-inspired "party of God." He issued a fatwa condemning the attack. Another condemnation came from Yusuf Qaradawi, a Qatar-based Egyptian television cleric with some fiery views and a following of millions.

All that is heartening. The trouble is that small groups can produce big consequences. Only 19 young men took part in the attacks of September 11th. But the 19 changed history. Their action led within two years to an American-led invasion and military occupation of two Muslim countries, Afghanistan and Iraq. This in turn has damaged Muslim perceptions of the United States, and perhaps by extension of the West at large.

A survey last June by the Pew Global Attitudes Project reported that negative views of America among Muslims had spread beyond the Middle East to Indonesia—the world's most populous Muslim country—and Nigeria. In many Muslim states a majority thought that America might become a military threat to their own country. Solid majorities of Palestinians and Indonesians—and nearly half of those in Morocco and Pakistan—said they had at least some confidence in Osama

bin Laden to "do the right thing regarding world affairs."
Seven out of ten Palestinians said they had confidence in
Mr. bin Laden in this regard.

Besides, it is not necessary for many Muslims to have
heard directly of people such as Qutb or Maudoodi or Abd
al-Wahhab in order for the world-view of such men to spread.
Some of the ideas of Abd al-Wahhab, for example, have been
embraced for generations by the Saudi Arabian state and,
more recently, disseminated to mosques far and wide on the
back of Saudi petrodollars. Wahhabism is a puritanical and
often anti-western Sunni doctrine, but the smaller Shia branch
of Islam is also exposed to extreme anti-western ideas, such
as those pumped out every Friday by mosques in Iran.

Where does all this leave the relationship between Islam
and Islamic terrorism? For the average Muslim Islam is
merely a religion, a way of organising life in accordance with
God's will. Is it a religion of peace or of violence? Like other
religions, it possesses holy texts that can be invoked to support either, depending on the circumstances. Like the Bible,
the Koran (which differs from the Bible in that Muslims take
all of it to be the word of God dictated directly to Muhammad,
his prophet) and the hadith contain injunctions both fiery and
pacific. Muslims are enjoined to show charity and compassion.
Yes, Islam has a concept of jihad (holy war), which some
Muslims think should be added to the five more familiar pillars
of faith: the oath of belief, prayer, charity, fasting, and pilgrimage. But the Koran also insists that there should be no
compulsion in religion.

Islam and Christendom have clashed for centuries. But if
there is something in the essence of Islam that predisposes its

adherents to violent conflict with the West, it is hard to say what it might be. The search for the something might anyway be an exercise in futility, given that the essentials of the faith are so hotly contested. Islam has no pope or equivalent central authority (though some Shias aspire to one). This means, as Oxford University's James Piscatori has argued, that the religious authorities and the official ulema find themselves in competition with unofficial or popular religious leaders and preachers, Sufi movements, Islamist groups, and lay intellectuals. "All of these and others claim direct access to scripture, purport to interpret its contemporary meaning, and thus effectively question whether any one individual or group has a monopoly on the sacred—even as they appropriate that right for themselves."

CHAPTER THREE

INDIVIDUAL DEVELOPMENT AND IDENTITY: OSAMA BIN LADEN AND IDEOLOGY

Published shortly after the attacks on the World Trade Center and the Pentagon, the following article from the Washington Post *traces the growth of bin Laden's resentment toward the United States and his long history of violence.*

Prior to 9/11, Osama bin Laden had been executing terrorist attacks against the United States, including the embassy bombings in East Africa (1998) and the attack on the USS Cole *stationed off the coast of Yemen (2000). In addition, after declaring a holy war against the United States in 1998, bin Laden was designated public enemy number one by the United States and was recognized as such by several other nations. However, no one predicted the scale to which his disdain for the United States would manifest itself on September 11, 2001.*

In this insightful article, veteran journalist Michael Dobbs draws on past interviews with bin Laden to depict bin Laden's worldview and how it is opposed to that of the vast majority of the American citizenry. —**AI**

"Inside the Mind of Osama bin Laden"
by Michael Dobbs
Washington Post, **September 20, 2001**

Several months after Osama bin Laden declared holy war on the United States in August 1996, an Arab journalist trekked up to his hide-out, 8,000 feet high in the mountains of southern Afghanistan. Why, he asked the fugitive Saudi millionaire and terrorism financier, had there been no immediate attacks to back up the threats?

"If we wanted to carry out small operations, it would have been easy to do," bin Laden told the reporter. "The nature of the battle requires good preparation."

In the 10 years before his emergence last week as the prime suspect in the deadliest terrorist attack in history, bin Laden, 44, has described his goals, grievances and tactics in great detail in a series of statements and interviews. Taken together, these statements provide insight into an ideology that seems abhorrent and even crazy to the vast majority of Americans but has been carefully crafted to appeal to the disgruntled and dispossessed of the Islamic world.

Elements of the attacks in New York and Washington were foreshadowed by bin Laden's explanations of his vision and methods. One of his themes, for example, is the importance of guerrilla warfare, as opposed to frontal combat with a more powerful enemy. Another is the need for lengthy preparation. Meticulous planning—sometimes for as long as three or four years—has been a hallmark of terrorist operations associated with bin Laden, including the 1998 bomb attacks on U.S.

embassies in East Africa and the destruction of the USS *Cole* in Aden, Yemen, last year.

At the heart of the bin Laden opus are two declarations of holy war—jihad—against America. The first, issued in 1996, was directed specifically at "Americans occupying the land of the two holy places," as bin Laden refers to his native Saudi Arabia, where 5,000 U.S. troops have been stationed since the 1991 Persian Gulf War. The two holy places are Muslim shrines at Mecca and Medina.

In 1998, he broadened the edict to include the killing of "Americans and their allies, civilians and military . . . in any country in which it is possible to do it."

Although the first attacks directly associated with bin Laden took place in Saudi Arabia, Somalia, East Africa and Yemen, he made clear all along that he planned to bring his war to the American homeland. The battle will "inevitably move . . . to American soil," he told *ABC News* reporter John Miller in May 1998, shortly after publication of the second edict.

In return for joining the jihad against America, bin Laden promises his followers an honored place in paradise, in accordance with the statement in the Koran that "a martyr's privileges are guaranteed by Allah." True Islamic youths, bin Laden argued in his 1996 decree, know that their rewards from fighting the United States will be "double" their rewards from fighting other countries. Their only aim in life, he has told Americans, is "to enter paradise by killing you."

Against U.S. Presence

The pivotal date in bin Laden's emergence as a sworn enemy of the United States is 1991, the year of the Persian Gulf War.

The son of a fabulously wealthy Saudi construction magnate, he had just returned home to Saudi Arabia after a decade fighting alongside the Afghan mujaheddin in their CIA-funded insurrection against the Soviet army. He was enraged to discover that "American crusader forces" were "occupying" his homeland.

In the American view, U.S. troops were in Saudi Arabia to liberate the neighboring state of Kuwait, which had been invaded by the armies of Iraqi leader Saddam Hussein. After the Gulf War ended, U.S. forces, which had not been stationed in Saudi Arabia before the war, remained on a semi-permanent basis to train the Saudi air force and police forces and protect the kingdom from further Iraqi mischief.

Bin Laden, along with an increasingly vocal Saudi opposition, saw the matter quite differently. In their view, the presence of foreign forces was an intolerable affront to 1,400 years of Islamic tradition, dating back to an injunction from the prophet Muhammad that there "not be two religions in Arabia." They argued that responsibility for defending the kingdom should fall on the Saudi government, which had poured billions of dollars into the military, rather than on Western "crusader forces."

Despite controlling 11 percent of the world's oil supply, Saudi Arabia was beginning to feel the effects of an increasingly serious economic crisis, caused by falling oil prices and widespread corruption. Bin Laden tied all this to the presence of foreign troops on Saudi soil and the "unjustified heavy spending on these forces" by the Saudi government. "The crusader forces became the main cause of our disastrous condition," he wrote in his 1996 declaration of jihad.

Two years later, in the 1998 decree, described by Islamic scholar Bernard Lewis of Princeton University as "a magnificent piece of eloquent, at times even poetic Arabic prose," bin Laden charged that Americans had declared war on Muslims. "For more than seven years the United States is occupying the lands of Islam in the holiest of its territories, Arabia, plundering its riches, overwhelming its rulers, humiliating its people, threatening its neighbors, and using its bases in the peninsula as a spearhead to fight against the neighboring Islamic peoples."

In bin Laden's war, the goal of expelling the "Judeo-Christian enemy" from the holy lands of Islam should be met first on the Arabian peninsula. His next priority is Iraq, which for 500 years was the seat of the most powerful Islamic state, or caliphate. A distant third on this agenda is Palestine, site of the al-Aqsa mosque in Jerusalem, which Muslims believe was the place where Muhammad ascended to heaven.

Bin Laden's view of America is almost the mirror opposite of America's view of him. In his opinion, he and his supporters are waging a just war against American "terrorism." Terrorist acts committed by Americans, according to bin Laden, include the "occupation" of Saudi Arabia, the "starving" of up to a million Iraqi children because of U.N. sanctions, the withholding of arms to Bosnian Muslims in their war against Christian Serbs, and the dropping of atomic bombs on Japan at the end of World War II.

Terrorism, bin Laden told *ABC News* in 1998, can be both "reprehensible" and "commendable."

"In today's wars," he said, "there are no morals. [Americans] rip us of our wealth and of our resources and of our oil. Our religion is under attack. They kill and murder our brothers. They compromise our honor and our dignity and dare we utter a single word of protest against the injustice, we are called terrorists."

Bin Laden's declarations of jihad draw on a radical interpretation of Islam that is contested by most Muslims. In medieval times, Islamic jurists differed on the moral permissibility of using poisoned arrows and poisoning enemy water supplies, what Lewis describes as "the missile and chemical warfare of the Middle Ages." But at no point, Lewis wrote in a 1998 article for *Foreign Affairs*, do basic Islamic texts even consider "the random slaughter of uninvolved bystanders."

Traditionally, responsibility for declaring a jihad rested with a community of scholars and theologians known as the ulema. But according to Khaled Abou el Fadl, an Islamic law expert at UCLA, the collapse of centralized authority in the Islamic world has led to a "moral and political vacuum" in which virtually any Muslim can declare a jihad. He added, however, that according to Islamic tradition, a religious decree, or fatwa, of the kind issued by bin Laden is "nonbinding" on other believers.

"Myth of the Superpower"

What Americans view as bin Laden's megalomania—the conviction that he and a relatively small band of followers can defeat a superpower—has its origins in the humbling of the Soviet superpower in the mountains of Afghanistan. In a CNN interview in 1997, he said that "the myth of the superpower was destroyed not only in my mind but also in the minds of all Muslims" as a result of the Soviet defeat in Afghanistan at the hands of mujaheddin.

Bin Laden's contempt for America seems even greater than his contempt for the Soviet Union. "The Russian soldier is more courageous and patient than the U.S. soldier," he told the London-based Arab newspaper, *al-Quds al-Arabi*, in 1996. "Our battle with the United States is easy compared with the battles in which we engaged in Afghanistan."

As examples of alleged American cowardice, bin Laden frequently cites the case of the withdrawal from Lebanon after the 1983 truck bombing of the Marine barracks in Beirut and the withdrawal from Somalia after the 1993 killings of U.S. servicemen in Mogadishu. Bin Laden also has paid a great deal of attention to the symbolism of his targets. In a video that circulated widely in the Arab world earlier this year, he bragged of the attack on the USS *Cole* by a boat filled with explosives in Aden harbor in October 2000. The destroyer had the "illusion she could destroy anything," but was itself destroyed by a tiny boat, bin Laden said.

"The destroyer represented the West, and the small boat represented Muhammad," he boasted, according to a transcript of the videotape supplied by Peter Bergen, author of *Holy War Inc.*, a forthcoming book about bin Laden.

———■———

A little less than two years before the September 11 attacks, Osama bin Laden gave an interview to Time Asia *magazine journalist Rahimullah Yusufzai. In the interview, bin Laden attested to his hatred for the United States and professed a moral duty to commit acts of terrorism against any nation or person he believes to be in opposition to the tenets of Islam. As in other interviews*

*and speeches, bin Laden is asked for his reaction to being
dubbed a terrorist by countries such as the United States
and its Middle Eastern ally Israel. As before, bin Laden
inverts the terrorist label and applies it to the United
States. He claims that the United States is a frail, terrorist nation, hiding behind the facade of a political and
economic superpower. He describes a type of "good" terrorism, which he sees as a defense of one's rights against
bullying nations that compromise Islamic traditions. —AI*

"Wrath of God"
Time Asia, January 11, 1999

Tall and lean, he was dressed in a traditional shalwar
kameez—baggy trousers and long shirt—under a military
fatigue jacket, with a scarf to fight the desert cold. An AK-47
assault rifle stood at his side. He spoke softly, in Arabic, prais-
ing God in nearly every sentence, but his voice rose whenever
he criticized the United States. That he did often during the
four-hour interview, his first since the U.S. tried to kill him.

Osama bin Laden, the Saudi financier accused of masterminding the Aug. 7 bombings that took 224 lives at two U.S.
embassies in Africa, escaped an American missile attack on
his headquarters in southern Afghanistan nearly two weeks
after the embassy blasts. In the months that followed, bin
Laden heeded the orders of his host, the Taliban militia that
controls most of Afghanistan, to avoid public statements. The
Taliban's leaders evidently didn't want to complicate their bud-
ding relations with the outside world. But last month's U.S.
bombing of Iraq evidently convinced them they had little to

lose from letting bin Laden talk. The exile himself wanted to deny involvement in the embassy bombings—and dispel rumors he is dying of cancer.

So late last month, bin Laden summoned Rahimullah Yusufzai, a well-connected journalist who reports for Pakistan's *The News*, as well as *Time* and *ABC News*, to his tented encampment in Afghanistan's Helmand province. Bin Laden has been on the move since the U.S. attack on his head-quarters, and he avoids using a satellite phone for fear it could betray his location. During Yusufzai's late-night conversation with bin Laden, the man the U.S. calls Public Enemy Number One appeared to be in good health, though he admitted to a sore throat and a bad back. He continually sipped water from a cup, and Yusufzai caught him on videotape walking with the aid of a stick (bodyguards erased that footage). Excerpts from the interview:

TIME: Are you responsible for the bomb attacks on the two U.S. embassies in Africa?

Osama bin Laden: The International Islamic Front for Jihad against the U.S. and Israel has issued a crystal-clear fatwa calling on the Islamic nation to carry on jihad aimed at liberating holy sites. The nation of Muhammad has responded to this appeal. If the instigation for jihad against the Jews and the Americans in order to liberate Al-Aksa Mosque and the Holy Ka'aba [Islamic shrines in the Middle East] is considered a crime, then let his-tory be a witness that I am a criminal. Our job is to instigate and, by the grace of God, we did that—and certain people responded to this instigation.

TIME: Do you know the men who have been arrested for these attacks?

Osama bin Laden: What I know is that those who risked their lives to earn the pleasure of God are real men. They managed to rid the Islamic nation of disgrace. We hold them in the highest esteem.

TIME: But all those arrested are said to have been associated with you.

Osama bin Laden: Wadih el-Hage was one of our brothers whom God was kind enough to steer to the path of relief work for Afghan refugees. I still remember him, though I have not seen him or heard from him for many years. He has nothing to do with the U.S. allegations. As for Mohamed Rashed al-'Owhali, we were informed that he is a Saudi from the province of Najd. Mamdouh Salim is a righteous man who memorizes the holy Koran. He was never a member of any jihad organization. The fact of the matter is that America, and in particular the CIA, wanted to cover up their failure in the aftermath of the events that took place in Riyadh, Nairobi, Dar es Salaam, Capetown, Kampala— and other places, God willing, in the future—by arresting any person who had participated in the Islamic jihad in Afghanistan. We pray to God to end the plight [of the arrested men], and we are confident they will be exonerated.

TIME: If the targets of jihad are Americans, how can you justify the deaths of Africans?

Osama bin Laden: This question pre-supposes that it is me who carried out these explosions. My answer is that I understand the motives of the brothers who act against the enemies of the nation. When it becomes apparent that it would be impossible to repel these Americans without assaulting them, even if this involved the killing of Muslims, this is permissible under Islam.

TIME: How do you react to the December attack on Iraq by U.S. and British forces?

Osama bin Laden: There is no doubt that the treacherous attack has confirmed that Britain and America are act-ing on behalf of Israel and the Jews, paving the way for the Jews to divide the Muslim world once again, enslave it and loot the rest of its wealth. A great part of the force that carried out the attack came from cer-tain Gulf countries that have lost their sovereignty. Now infidels walk everywhere on the land where Muhammad was born and where the Koran was revealed to him. The situation is serious. The rulers have become powerless. Muslims should carry out their obligations, since the rulers of the region have accepted the invasion of their countries. These coun-tries belong to Islam and not to the rulers.

TIME: What can the U.S. expect from you now?

Osama bin Laden: Any thief or criminal or robber who enters another country in order to steal should expect to be exposed to murder at any time. For the American forces to expect anything from me, personally, reflects a very narrow perception. Muslims are angry. The Americans should expect reactions from the Muslim world that are proportionate to the injustice they inflict.

TIME: The U.S. says you are trying to acquire chemical and nuclear weapons. How would you use these?

Osama bin Laden: Acquiring weapons for the defense of Muslims is a religious duty. If I have indeed acquired these weapons, then I thank God for enabling me to do so. And if I seek to acquire these weapons, I am carrying out a duty. It would be a sin for Muslims not to try to possess the weapons that would prevent the infidels from inflicting harm on Muslims.

TIME: Can you describe the U.S. air strikes on your camps?

Osama bin Laden: The American bombardment had only shown that the world is governed by the law of the jungle. That brutal, treacherous attack killed a number of civilian Muslims. As for material damage, it was minimal. By the grace of God, the missiles were ineffective. The raid proved that the American army is going downhill in its morale. Its members are too cowardly and too fearful to meet the young people of Islam face to face.

TIME: The U.S. is trying to stop the flow of funds to your organization. Has it been able to do so?

Osama bin Laden: The U.S. knows that I have attacked it, by the grace of God, for more than ten years now. The

U.S. alleges that I am fully responsible for the killing of its soldiers in Somalia. God knows that we have been pleased at the killing of American soldiers. This was achieved by the grace of God and the efforts of the mujahedin from among the Somali brothers and other Arab mujahedin who had been in Afghanistan before that. America has been trying ever since to tighten its economic blockade against us and to arrest me. It has failed. This blockade does not hurt us much. We expect to be rewarded by God.

TIME: What will you do if the Taliban asks you to leave Afghanistan?

Osama bin Laden: That is not something we foresee. We do not expect to be driven out of this land. We pray to God to make our migration a migration in His cause.

TIME: Do you expect any more attacks if you stay in Afghanistan?

Osama bin Laden: Any foreign attack on Afghanistan would not target an individual. It would not target Osama bin Laden personally. The fact is that Afghanistan, having raised the banner of Islam, has become a target for the crusader-Jewish alliance. We expect Afghanistan to be bombarded, even though the non-believers will say that they do so because of the presence of Osama. That is why we, together with our brothers, live on these mountains far away from Muslims in villages and towns, in order to spare them any harm.

TIME: Is your Islamic message having an impact?

Osama bin Laden: Winds ot change have blown in order to lift the injustice to which the world is subjected by America and its supporters and the Jews who are collaborating with them. Look at what is happening these days in Indonesia, where Suharto, a despot who ruled for 30 years, was overthrown. During his reign, the media glorified him, depicting him as the best president. The media in the Arab countries, regrettably, is doing the same these days. But things will change. The time will come, sooner rather than later, when criminal despots who betrayed God and His Prophet, and betrayed their trust and their nation, will face the same fate.

TIME: But there are many Muslims who do not agree with your kind of violence.

Osama bin Laden: We should fully understand our religion. Fighting is a part of our religion and our Shari'a. Those who love God and his Prophet and this religion cannot deny that. Whoever denies even a minor tenet of our religion commits the gravest sin in Islam. Those who sympathize with the infidels—such as the PLO in Palestine, or the so-called Palestinian Authority—have been trying for tens of years to get back some of their rights. They laid down arms and abandoned what is called "violence" and tried peaceful bargaining. What did the Jews give them? They did not give them even 1% of their rights.

TIME: America, the world's only superpower, has called you Public Enemy Number One. Are you worried?

Osama bin Laden: Hostility toward America is a religious duty, and we hope to be rewarded for it by God. To call us Enemy Number One or Two does not hurt us. Osama bin Laden is confident that the Islamic nation will carry out its duty. I am confident that Muslims will be able to end the legend of the so-called superpower that is America.

———◻———

During the 2004 U.S. presidential elections, Aljazeera TV, an Arabic network based out of Qatar, released a video message from Osama bin Laden. Evidence that bin Laden was still alive had not surfaced for more than a year, and reports that bin Laden suffered from kidney failure left many people wondering if he was, in fact, still alive.

The video is significant for a number of reasons. Most important, it is the first time that bin Laden publicly admits to masterminding the 9/11 attacks against the United States. Also, bin Laden vehemently attacks the Bush administration in the video, which appeared only four days before the 2004 U.S. presidential elections. The language and tone taunts the president, quite possibly in an attempt to convince American citizens to begin to doubt and turn against their leader.

The title of this piece includes an alternate spelling of bin Laden's name: Usama bin Ladin. Often in translating Arabic words and names to English, there is some variation in spelling due to preferences of the translator.

This variation can also be seen in the alternate spellings of "Al Qaeda," such as "al-Qaida." —AI

"Excerpts from Usama bin Ladin's Speech"
Aljazeera.net, October 29, 2004

"O American people, I am speaking to tell you about the ideal way to avoid another Manhattan, about war and its causes and results.

"Security is an important foundation of human life and free people do not squander their security, contrary to Bush's claims that we hate freedom. Let him tell us why we did not attack Sweden for example.

"It is known that those who hate freedom do not possess proud souls like those of the 19, may God rest their souls. We fought you because we are free and because we want freedom for our nation. When you squander our security we squander yours.

"I am surprised by you. Despite entering the fourth year after September 11, Bush is still deceiving you and hiding the truth from you and therefore the reasons are still there to repeat what happened.

"God knows it did not cross our minds to attack the towers but after the situation became unbearable and we witnessed the injustice and tyranny of the American-Israeli alliance against our people in Palestine and Lebanon, I thought about it. And the events that affected me directly were that of 1982 and the events

that followed—when America allowed the Israelis to invade Lebanon, helped by the US Sixth Fleet.

"In those difficult moments many emotions came over me which are hard to describe, but which produced an overwhelming feeling to reject injustice and a strong determination to punish the unjust.

"As I watched the destroyed towers in Lebanon, it occurred to me [to] punish the unjust the same way [and] to destroy towers in America so it could taste some of what we are tasting and to stop killing our children and women.

"We had no difficulty in dealing with Bush and his administration because they resemble the regimes in our countries, half of which are ruled by the military and the other half by the sons of kings . . . They have a lot of pride, arrogance, greed and thievery.

"He [Bush] adopted despotism and the crushing of freedoms from Arab rulers and called it the Patriot Act under the guise of combating terrorism.

"We had agreed with the [September 11] overall commander Muhammad Atta, may God rest his soul, to carry out all operations in 20 minutes before Bush and his administration take notice.

"It never occurred to us that the commander in chief of the American forces [Bush] would leave 50,000 citizens in the two towers to face those horrors alone at a time when they most needed him because he thought listening to a child discussing her goat and its ramming was more important than the planes

and their ramming of the skyscrapers. This had given us three times the time needed to carry out the operations, thanks be to God.

"Your security is not in the hands of [Democratic presidential candidate John] Kerry or Bush or al-Qaida. Your security is in your own hands and each state which does not harm our security will remain safe."

———————■———————

Years have passed since 9/11 and Osama bin Laden still remains at large. Controversy abounds as to whether or not America has done all it can to apprehend bin Laden and bring him to justice. Many claim the war in Iraq diverged from the primary task of capturing bin Laden, while others think that bin Laden's capture is irrelevant.

Peter Bergen, the author of Holy War, Inc. (excerpted in chapter 1), has devoted several years to researching bin Laden and his terrorist network. Determined to uncover the details of the United States' search for bin Laden, he ventures to Afghanistan and Pakistan to trace the footsteps of the elusive terrorist since 9/11. During his investigation, he interviews more than two dozen American, Afghan, and Pakistani officials. He also speaks to a number of people who have met bin Laden. From these sources, he speculates on where bin Laden might be hiding and on various strategies the United States might use to find him. —AI

From "The Long Hunt for Osama"
by Peter Bergen
Atlantic Monthly, October 2004

. . . Why is it so hard to find Osama bin Laden? First, there is his obsession with security, which began in earnest not after 9/11 but a decade ago. In 1994, while bin Laden was living in Sudan, he was the target of a serious assassination attempt, possibly mounted by the Saudis, when a group of gunmen raked his Khartoum residence with machine-gun fire. After that attack bin Laden took much greater care of his security—an effort that was coordinated by Ali Mohamed, an Egyptian-American U.S. Army sergeant who during the late 1980s had worked as an instructor at U.S. Special Forces headquarters, at Fort Bragg, in North Carolina.

In 1997, when I was a producer for CNN, I met with bin Laden in eastern Afghanistan to film his first-ever television interview, and thus witnessed the extraordinary lengths to which members of al-Qaeda went to protect their leader. My colleagues and I were taken to bin Laden's hideout in the middle of the night; we were made to change vehicles while blindfolded; we were aggressively searched and electronically swept for tracking devices; and we had to pass through three successive groups of guards armed with submachine guns and rocket-propelled grenades.

As has often been observed, the leadership of al-Qaeda is highly secretive, running the organization in a compartmental-ized manner, which makes it hard to penetrate—and also ensures that any operative who may be captured will know only a portion of the group's secrets. An illustration of this is the limited number of al-Qaeda leaders who knew of the 9/11 plot. In a videotape discovered by U.S. forces in Afghanistan after the fall of the Taliban, bin Laden is seen gesturing at Sulaiman Abu Ghaith, then the group's spokesman, and observing that not even Abu Ghaith was clued in on 9/11. And it's worth recalling that bin Laden and al-Zawahiri [bin Laden's chief deputy] have spent their entire adult lives in organizations that prize discipline and secrecy. Al-Zawahiri joined a jihadist cell in Egypt when he was only fifteen; bin Laden became involved in clandestine efforts against the Soviets in Afghanistan when he was in his early twenties.

The situation is further complicated if bin Laden and al-Zawahiri are indeed hiding out in the tribal areas of Pakistan on the Afghan border—"the most concentrated al-Qaeda area on the planet," one American intelligence official told me. The Pakistan-Afghan border stretches 1,500 miles—roughly the distance from Washington, D.C., to Denver. It is lightly guarded and even undefined in some places; clandestine travel in the region is therefore relatively easy. The two Pakistani provinces that abut Afghanistan are Baluchistan, a vast, inhospitable expanse of broiling deserts, and the North West Frontier Province, a flinty, mountainous region punctuated by the fortresses of tribal chiefs. Pashtun tribes, who constitute one of the largest tribal groups in the world, are a major presence in both provinces. They subscribe to Pashtunwali, the law of the Pashtuns, which places an enormous premium on hospitality and on the giving of refuge to anybody who seeks it—an obvious boon to fugitive members of al-Qaeda.

But there's a problem with hiding somewhere along the Afghanistan-Pakistan frontier, according to Rahimullah

Yusufzai, a prominent Pashtun journalist. "Everybody knows everybody there," he told me. "If someone comes there who is from a different tribe, they stick out. It's difficult for Arabs to hide in tribal areas." If bin Laden and al-Zawahiri are indeed in Baluchistan or the North West Frontier, therefore, they may be hiding outside the remote tribal belt, in a city such as Peshawar or Quetta, or in a town such as Kohat or Dera Ismail Khan.

A further possibility, which to date has received scant attention, is that bin Laden is somewhere in the mountains of Pakistani Kashmir—an area that is off limits to outsiders and home to numerous Kashmiri militant groups, some of which are deeply intertwined with al-Qaeda. Harakat ul-Mujahideen (HUM), for instance, shared training camps in Afghanistan with al-Qaeda in the late 1990s. An offshoot of HUM, Jaish-e-Muhammad, orchestrated the kidnapping-murder of the American journalist Daniel Pearl in 2002, an operation run in conjunction with al-Qaeda. U.S. officials believe that Jaish-e-Muhammad received funding from bin Laden. The multiple relationships between those groups and al-Qaeda—what one U.S. official in the region described to me as "overlapping networks of nasty people"—make the groups obvious potential allies in the effort to hide bin Laden and al-Zawahiri. According to Pakistani terrorism analysts, several of the most militant Pakistani groups have recently gathered under an umbrella organization called Brigade 313, named for the number of men who stood with the Prophet Muhammad at the key battle of Badr, in the seventh century. Also, the Kashmiri militant groups are genuinely popular in Pakistan. Until January of 2002, when it was officially banned, Lashkar-e-Taiba maintained

2,200 offices around the country and attracted hundreds of thousands of followers to its annual gatherings. Technically Lashkar no longer exists, but it continues to operate, under a different name and with a lower profile, and its leader, Hafiz Saeed, continues to address rallies in Pakistan.

Further complicating the picture, the Pakistani government has long had a close relationship with the Kashmiri groups because they share the goal of expelling Indian forces from the Kashmir region. Bin Laden understands that Kashmir is Pakistan's "blind spot," a senior U.S. military-intelligence official told me. Musharraf's government has cracked down on Kashmiri militants since 9/11, but the intensity of the crackdown has ebbed and flowed. For instance, Maulana Masood Azhar, the leader of the Jaish terror group, is not under house arrest and, according to a U.S. official, has "good relations with [Pakistan's] spooks." An official in Afghanistan's Foreign Ministry concurs: "The leadership and brains of al-Qaeda are not in the tribal areas of Pakistan. The question is, Who is in Kashmir?"

To the extent that al-Qaeda has set up a new base of operations, it is neither in Afghanistan nor along the Afghan-Pakistani border but in the anonymity of Pakistan's teeming cities. As Lieutenant General Assad Durrani, the former head of Pakistan's ISI [Inter-Services Intelligence], explained to me "Cities offer the best refuge. In the countryside information gets leaked out more easily." Since 9/11 none of the key captured al-Qaeda operatives have been found in Pakistan's tribal areas; instead they have been run to ground in the cities of Karachi, Peshawar, Quetta, Faisalabad, Gujrat, and

Rawalpindi. Those arrested include Ramzi bin al-Shibh who was critical to the planning of 9/11; Abu Zubaydah, who recruited for al-Qaeda; Walid bin Attash, who played an important role in the attack on the U.S.S. *Cole* in Yemen; Ahmed Khalfan Ghailani, who is one of the conspirators in the 1998 bombing of the U.S. embassies in Kenya and Tanzania; Mustafa Ahmed al-Hawsawi, who bankrolled the 9/11 hijackers; and, most important, Khalid Sheikh Muhammad, the military commander of al-Qaeda, who had overall responsibility for planning the 9/11 attacks.

. . . In particular Karachi, a barely governable megacity of 14 million people, has emerged as a locus of jihadist violence perpetrated by a toxic alliance of the Kashmiri militant groups, Sunni sectarian fanatics who have launched a war on Pakistan's minority Shia, and al-Qaeda itself. Since 9/11 Karachi has experienced the bombing of a Sheraton hotel, which killed eleven French defense contractors; two separate attacks on the U.S. consulate, one of which killed a dozen Pakistanis; multiple bombings of Shell gas stations; and the murder of Daniel Pearl. In May alone militants killed sixty-three people in the city.

Al-Qaeda's active presence in Pakistan raises an important question: How reliable is the Pakistani government in the effort to hunt down the terrorist group? U.S. sources say that certain elements in the ISI may retain some ideological sympathy for the Taliban. However, the consistent record of high-profile al-Qaeda arrests in Pakistan indicates that the Pakistanis are doing a reasonably diligent job. According to Major General Shaukat Sultan Khan, the spokesman for the ISI, Pakistan has arrested 500 "foreign fighters" since 9/11.

Moreover, after the assassination attempts against him Musharraf is personally determined to destroy al-Qaeda. Nevertheless, lower-level members of the military were involved in the planning of those assassination attempts: up to four members of the army and six members of the air force, according to Khan.

The capture of Khalid Sheikh Muhammad, in March of 2003, was the most important al-Qaeda arrest since 9/11. However, according to Syed Mohsin Naqvi, a Pakistani journalist who interviewed Muhammad while he was on the run in August of 2002, Muhammad claimed that others were ready to replace him in the event he was arrested. "We already have so many backups," he said, "that the Americans can't imagine."

Muhammad's arrest may have brought investigators tantalizingly close to bin Laden himself. According to American sources, when Muhammad was arrested he may have been tortured, a not uncommon technique of Pakistani law enforcement. That may explain why he quickly volunteered that he had met with bin Laden in December of 2002. Although Muhammad would not reveal where the meeting took place, it was probably in Pakistan. After Muhammad's capture there was a brief flurry of anticipation that bin Laden himself would soon be arrested, but now, according to one U.S. official, bin Laden's "personal signature trail is cold."

A few months after the apprehension of Muhammad, I talked with Cofer Black, the former head of the CIA's Counterterrorist Center, who has something of a personal interest in tracking down bin Laden. In his spacious office at the State Department, where he is now serving as ambassador for counterterrorism, Black told me that while he was the CIA station chief in Sudan, during the mid-1990s, al-Qaeda tried to assassinate him. He handled the episode with admirable sangfroid, deciding to consider the attempt an exercise to "see how they [al-Qaeda] were conducting themselves." After 9/11, Black famously told President Bush that his operatives would bring Bush bin Laden's head "in a box." (A member of Black's staff told me that when his words came out in the press, Black said with a deadpan look, "Well, we will need some DNA.")

Black began our conversation by observing that the war on terrorism is far larger than the hunt for bin Laden. "You can't stop crime just by catching Al Capone," he said, going on to stress that he was not personally obsessed with getting bin Laden: "This is no Ahab and Moby Dick kind of deal." Bin Laden "is on the run, he is very defensive, spending a lot of time worrying about security," Black continued. "How effective can you be?" To avoid being captured bin Laden has to adopt a "hermit on the hilltop" approach, Black said, which destroys his ability to run an effective terrorist organization. On the other hand, if he remains "in business," he opens himself to the possibility that his communications will be detected. I suggested that bin Laden seems to be caught between a rock and a hard place, and Black leaned toward me, smiling broadly, and said, "You got it."

This past January, Lieutenant Colonel Brian Hilferty, the senior spokesman for U.S. forces in Afghanistan, announced, "We're sure we're going to catch Osama bin Laden and [the former Taliban leader] Mullah Omar this year." His prediction came at about the same time that the U.S. and Pakistani governments announced a plan to conduct more-intensive operations to find bin Laden. The joint "hammer-and-anvil" strategy involved Pakistan's moving 70,000 soldiers into the tribal regions to flush out al-Qaeda forces, which would then, at least theoretically, flee across the border into the arms of U.S. forces waiting for them on the Afghan side. But the plan was trumpeted at every turn—and as a result, any al-Qaeda member with an ounce of common sense very probably left the tribal areas earlier this year. "Al-Qaeda are not so foolish that they would be sitting waiting there for a year for the Pakistan army," Syed Mohsin Naqvi told me.

. . . Given that al-Qaeda is highly secretive, compartmentalized, and security conscious, what strategies might work to flush out bin Laden? Will the $50 million bounty on his head work? In the past cash rewards have been useful in bringing terrorists to justice. Mir Aimal Kansi, a Pakistani who killed two CIA employees outside the Agency's headquarters in Virginia in 1993, was apprehended in part because of the $2 million reward offered. A $25 million reward played a role in the apprehension of Khalid Sheikh Muhammad. However, these men did not inspire the spiritual awe that Osama bin Laden does. That bin Laden's inner circle would turn him over for money is unthinkable. Bin Laden has had a multi-million-dollar bounty on his head since as far back as 1999, but there have been no takers.

In Washington I met one of the FBI's most effective investigators, Special Agent Brad Garrett, who ran Mir Aimal Kansi to ground in Pakistan in 1997. I asked Garrett, a former Marine who habitually dresses entirely in black, what methods had worked to find Kansi, and how they might be applicable in the hunt for bin Laden. "The key is developing sources," Garrett said. "You have to sort out what is BS from what is the truth, and develop multiple sources to see what is real. You hope to get an associate to give up real-time information about the fugitive. The intelligence is very perishable, so another factor is one's ability to react to it in a timely fashion."

Garrett encountered many dry holes in his four-year hunt for Kansi, finally tracking him down in the dusty backwater of Dera Ghazi Khan, in central Pakistan, which "felt like it was out of *The Good, the Bad, and the Ugly.*" Garrett explained that although Kansi was helped by a loose network of people who "respected" him for his attack outside CIA headquarters, he did not have an organization he could rely on, as bin Laden does. In short, Kansi was more vulnerable to detection than the terrorist mastermind, because he was essentially a lone wolf.

. . . Information obtained from al-Qaeda detainees has proved important in the hunt for the group's leaders, as have the cell-phone numbers, documents, and computers recovered when al-Qaeda members are captured. U.S. intelligence services have apparently failed, however, to insert agents in al-Qaeda's inner circle—the only sure-fire way to get real-time intelligence about bin Laden's whereabouts. Colonel Patrick Lang, a fluent Arabic-speaker who ran Middle Eastern "humint" (human intelligence) for the Defense Intelligence Agency in the early 1990s, told me that the lack of humint remains a problem. "Everybody talks about effective humint," he said, "but nothing is happening. The people who do this kind of work are gifted eccentrics, who the bureaucrats don't like, or they are the criminal types, who the lawyers don't like. If only we were the ruthless bastards everyone thinks we are." According to the Pakistani terrorism analyst Amir Mir, however, the past year or so has produced one promising humint development: FBI officials have created what is known as the Spider Group—an elite team of retired Pakistani army and intelligence officers who are gathering information about the Taliban and al-Qaeda.

No matter how many resources are directed at the hunt for bin Laden, it is complicated by what one could call "the problem of finding one person." Criminals often stay on the FBI's Ten Most Wanted list for years. Eric Rudolph, the alleged bomber of Atlanta's Centennial Park during the 1996 Olympics, eluded the police during the most intense manhunt in FBI history and was caught only last year, in the small town of Murphy, North Carolina, when an alert rookie cop spotted him and took him in for questioning.

The problem of finding one person becomes more pro-nounced once the hunt is extended overseas, of course. For almost a decade the United States and its NATO allies have searched the former Yugoslavia for Radovan Karadzic and Ratko Mladic, both alleged to have played a key role in the genocide of Bosnian Muslims during the early 1990s. "The last time we got a sniff of Karadzic," a U.S. military official told me, "was in 1997." During Operation Restore Hope, a 1993 humanitarian mission to feed starving Somalis, the United States had some 20,000 soldiers stationed in Mogadishu, the Somali capital, hunting for Muhammad Aideed, a warlord who was fomenting factional strife in Somalia. Aideed was never captured.

Of course, the capture of Saddam Hussein is an example of a successful U.S. operation against a high-value target. However, the search for Saddam played out against a different backdrop: the United States has some 140,000 soldiers in

Iraq; it has only 20,000 in Afghanistan, a much larger country. And in Pakistan, where bin Laden is most probably hiding, the United States has only a smattering of CIA and FBI officials hunting for members of al-Qaeda, and must rely on the Pakistani army for search operations. Moreover, once Saddam's reign of fear collapsed, there were relatively few Saddam loyalists; in contrast, "love" is not too strong a word for the feelings of those who surround bin Laden. The former senior U.S. counterterrorism official Roger Cressey told me that an al-Qaeda operative betraying bin Laden would be like "a Catholic giving up the Pope."

If cash rewards, electronic intercepts, and moles within al-Qaeda are unlikely to yield leads in the search for bin Laden, then what might work, other than dumb luck? An obvious vulnerability is the audiotapes that bin Laden and al-Zawahiri periodically release to media outlets; theoretically, the custody chain of these tapes could be traced back to al-Qaeda's leaders. Another possible vulnerability is bin Laden's family. He is the only son of his Syrian mother, to whom he is extremely close and who visited Afghanistan in early 2001 to attend the wedding of one of her grandsons. She apparently splits her time between Saudi Arabia and the resort town of Latakia, Syria, and is presumably of considerable interest to investigative agencies.

Bin Laden also has a family of four wives and some twenty children, who cannot all have simply vanished into thin air. Although some of his children are living openly in Saudi Arabia, others are quite possibly somewhere in Afghanistan, probably under the protection of key Taliban commanders close to bin Laden. The person protecting bin Laden's family may be Jalaluddin Haqqani, a formidable Taliban commander who continues to attack American forces in eastern Afghanistan. Haqqani may be a key to finding bin Laden.

One of the most effective Afghan commanders against the Soviets, Haqqani was close to the Arab militants who were drawn to the Afghan jihad. He is married to an Arab, speaks fluent Arabic, and received substantial funding from sources in the Gulf during the early 1980s, which he used to set up an impressive base in the Khost area of eastern Afghanistan. After 9/11 Haqqani was tapped to become the Taliban's military commander. Lutfullah Mashal, of the Afghan Interior Ministry, told me that it was Haqqani who saved bin Laden after the fall of the Taliban, affording him refuge in Khost not long after the terrorist leader had slipped out of Tora Bora. According to Mashal, Haqqani is now based in Pakistan, in the wild tribal area of Waziristan, traveling back and forth more or less at will. According to Afghan and American officials, he remains an important point of contact for al-Qaeda's leaders.

Another veteran commander of the Afghan war against the Soviets who is close to bin Laden and therefore merits further investigation is Younis Khalis. When bin Laden settled in Jalalabad, in May of 1996, he was welcomed not by the Taliban, who as yet did not control Jalalabad, but by Khalis. Khalis has repeatedly declared a *jihad* against U.S. forces in Afghanistan, most recently this past summer.

. . . Osama bin Laden may eventually be apprehended, or he may eventually be killed. A U.S. intelligence official told me that little thought has been given in Washington to what happens next. Which outcome is more desirable? What are the implications of either of those outcomes? If bin Laden is captured alive, for instance, where should he be put on trial? A case could be made that he be tried by an international tribunal, similar to those set up for crimes against humanity in the former Yugoslavia and Rwanda. And a useful precedent exists for handling a captured bin Laden: the pictures beamed around the world after Saddam Hussein's capture, of Saddam submitting to a doctor's probings, did more than anything else to puncture the Iraqi dictator's mystique. Similar pictures would do much to deflate bin Laden's mythic persona.

Of course, on several occasions bin Laden has said that he's prepared to die in his holy war—a statement that should be taken at face value. Khalid Khawaja, the former Pakistani military-intelligence official who has known bin Laden for almost two decades, told me, "He will never be captured. He's not Saddam Hussein. He's Osama. Osama loves death." In the short term bin Laden's death would probably trigger violent anti-American attacks around the globe. In the medium term it would be a serious blow to al-Qaeda, which depends to a critical degree on the charisma of its leader. But in the long term bin Laden's "martyrdom" would most likely give an enormous boost to the power of his ideas. Sayyid Qutb, generally regarded as the Lenin of the jihadist movement, was a relatively obscure writer before the Egyptian government executed him, in 1966. After his death his writings, which called for offensive holy wars against the enemies of Islam, became enormously influential. The same thing would happen after bin Laden's death, but to an infinitely greater degree.

CHAPTER FOUR

POWER, AUTHORITY, AND GOVERNANCE: AL QAEDA AND THE UNITED STATES

In autumn of 2001, Alan Cullison was covering the war against the Taliban in Afghanistan for the Wall Street Journal. *When his computer was destroyed in a car accident, he sought out a computer dealer in downtown Kabul for a replacement. Computer dealers were hard to find in the war-ravaged city, but Cullison eventually located someone who was willing to sell him a desktop computer and a laptop computer for $1,100. Supposedly, the seller had stolen the computers from Al Qaeda's central office after Al Qaeda leaders had fled in haste.*

To Cullison's surprise, the computers really had been owned by Al Qaeda. Cullison found, saved on the desktop computer's hard drive, thousands of files created by Al Qaeda members, including Ayman al-Zawahiri, Osama bin Laden's top deputy. Before handing the computers over to the CIA, Cullison had copies of the files made. Excerpts from these files are included in the following selection from Atlantic Monthly *magazine. —AI*

From "Inside Al-Qaeda's Hard Drive"
by Alan Cullison
Atlantic Monthly, **September 2004**

. . . Al-Qaeda's leaders began decamping to Afghanistan
in 1996, after the group was expelled from Sudan. Ayman
al-Zawahiri, at the time also the leader of the militant Egyptian group Islamic Jihad, issued a call for other Islamists to
follow, and in one letter found on the computer described
Afghanistan as a "den of garrisoned lions." But not all Arabs
were happy with the move. Afghanistan, racked by more
than a decade of civil war and Soviet occupation, struck
many as unfit to be the capital of global jihad. Jihadis com-
plained about the food, the bad roads, and the Afghans
themselves, who, they said, were uneducated, venal, and not
to be trusted.

. . . The Arabs' general contempt for the backwardness
of Afghanistan was not lost on the Taliban, whose leaders
grew annoyed with Osama bin Laden's focus on public relations and the media. Letters found on the computer reveal that
relations between the Arabs and the Taliban had grown so
tense that many feared the Taliban leader, Mullah Muhammad
Omar, would expel the Arabs from the country. A dialogue to
resolve the two sides' differences was carried on at the highest levels, as the memo below, from two Syrian operatives,
demonstrates. ("Abu Abdullah" is a code name for bin Laden;
"Leader of the Faithful" refers to Mullah Omar, in his hoped-
for capacity as the head of a new Islamic emirate, based in
Afghanistan.)

To: Osama bin Laden
From: Abu Mosab al-Suri and Abu Khalid al-Suri
Via: Ayman al-Zawahiri
Folder: Incoming Mail—From Afghanistan
Date: July 19, 1999

Noble brother Abu Abdullah,
Peace upon you, and God's mercy and blessings.
This message [concerns] the problem between you
and the Leader of the Faithful . . .

The results of this crisis can be felt even here in Kabul and other
places. Talk about closing down the camps has spread. Discontent
with the Arabs has become clear. Whispers between the Taliban
with some of our non-Arab brothers has become customary. In
short, our brother Abu Abdullah's latest troublemaking with the
Taliban and the Leader of the Faithful jeopardizes the Arabs,
and the Arab presence, today in all of Afghanistan, for no good
reason. It provides a ripe opportunity for all adversaries, includ-
ing America, the West, the Jews, Saudi Arabia, Pakistan, the
Mas'ud-Dostum alliance, etc., to serve the Arabs a blow that
could end up causing their most faithful allies to kick them out
. . . Our brother [bin Laden] will help our enemies reach their
goal free of charge! . . .

   The strangest thing I have heard so far is Abu Abdullah's
saying that he wouldn't listen to the Leader of the Faithful when
he asked him to stop giving interviews . . . I think our brother
[bin Laden] has caught the disease of screens, flashes, fans, and
applause . . .

The only solution out of this dilemma is what a number of knowledgeable and experienced people have agreed upon . . .

Abu Abdullah should go to the Leader of the Faithful with some of his brothers and tell them that . . . the Leader of the Faithful was right when he asked you to refrain from interviews, announcements, and media encounters, and that you will help the Taliban as much as you can in their battle, until they achieve control over Afghanistan. . . . You should apologize for any inconvenience or pressure you have caused . . . and commit to the wishes and orders of the Leader of the Faithful on matters that concern his circumstances here . . .

The Leader of the Faithful, who should be obeyed where he reigns, is Muhammad Omar, not Osama bin Laden. Osama bin Laden and his companions are only guests seeking refuge and have to adhere to the terms laid out by the person who provided it for them. This is legitimate and logical.

The troubled relationship between al-Qaeda and the Taliban hadn't interfered with global plans. Al-Qaeda had developed a growing interest in suicide operations as an offensive weapon against Americans and other enemies around the world. On August 7, 1998, the group simultaneously struck the U.S. embassies in Kenya and Tanzania with car bombs, killing more than 220 people and wounding more than 4,000. Concerned that inflicting such heavy casualties on civilians would tarnish its image even among its supporters, al-Qaeda actively sought religious and legal opinions from Islamic scholars around the world who could help to justify the killing of innocents. The following letter is presumably a typical request for theological guidance.

To: Unknown
From: Unknown
Folder: Outgoing Mail
Date: September 26, 1998

Dear highly respected _____

. . . I present this to you as your humble brother . . . concerning the preparation of the lawful study that I am doing on the killing of civilians. This is a very sensitive case—as you know—especially these days . . .

It is very important that you provide your opinion of this matter, which has been forced upon us as an essential issue in the course and ideology of the Muslim movement . . .

[Our] questions are:

1. *Since you are the representative of the Islamic Jihad group, what is your lawful stand on the killing of civilians, specifically when women and children are included? And please explain the legitimate law concerning those who are deliberately killed.*
2. *According to your law, how can you justify the killing of innocent victims because of a claim of oppression?*
3. *What is your stand concerning a group that supports the killing of civilians, including women and children?*

With our prayers, wishing you success and stability.

Secret Operations

As al-Qaeda established itself in Afghanistan in the late 1990s and began managing international operations of ever increasing complexity and audacity, the group focused on ensuring the secrecy of its communications. It discouraged the use of e-mail and the telephone, and recommended faxes and couriers. The electronic files reflect the global nature of the work being done; much of the correspondence was neatly filed by country name. Messages were usually encrypted and often couched in language mimicking that of a multinational corporation; thus Osama bin Laden was sometimes "the contractor," acts of terrorism became "trade," Mullah Omar and the Taliban became "the Omar Brothers Company," the security services of the United States and Great Britain became "foreign competitors," and so on. Especially sensitive messages were encoded with a simple but reliable cryptographic system that had been used by both Allied and Axis powers during World War II—a "one-time pad" system that paired individual letters with randomly assigned numbers and letters and produced messages readable only by those who knew the pairings. The computer's files reveal that in 1998 and 1999, when a number of Islamists connected to al-Qaeda were arrested or compromised abroad, the jihadis in Afghanistan relied heavily on the one-time-pad system. They also devised new code names for people and places.

Letters sent from and to Ayman al-Zawahiri in 1999 contain coded language typical of many files on the computer; they also show the degree to which al-Qaeda operatives abroad were being exposed and detained because of their efforts. In the first of the following two letters much of the code remains mysterious.

To: Yemen Cell Members
From: Ayman al-Zawahiri

Folder: Outgoing Mail—To Yemen
Date: February 1, 1999

. . . I would like to clarify the following with relation to the birth-day [probably an unspecified attack]:

a) *Don't think of showering as it may harm your health.*

b) *We can't make a hotel reservation for you, but they usually don't mind making reservations for guests. Those who wish to make a reservation should go to Quwedar [a famous pastry shop in Cairo].*

c) *I suggest that each of you takes a recipient to Quwedar to buy sweets, then make the hotel reservation. It is easy. After you check in, walk to Nur. After you attend the birthday go from Quwedar to Bushra St., where you should buy movie tickets to the Za'bolla movie theater.*

d) *The birthday will be in the third month. How do you want to celebrate it in the seventh? Do you want us to change the boy's birth date? There are guests awaiting the real date to get back to their work.*

e) *I don't have any gravel [probably ammunition or bomb-making material].*

To: Ayman al-Zawahiri
From: Unknown
Folder: Incoming Mail—From Yemen
Date: May 13, 1999

Dear brother Salah al-Din:

. . . Forty of the contractor's [bin Laden's] friends here were taken by surprise by malaria [arrested] a few days ago, following

the telegram they sent, which was similar to Salah al-Din's telegrams [that is, it used the same code]. The majority of them are from here [Yemen], and two are from the contractor's country [Saudi Arabia] . . .

We heard that al-Asmar had a sudden illness and went to the hospital [prison]. He will have a session with the doctors [lawyers] early next month to see if he can be treated there, or if he should be sent for treatment in his country [probably Egypt, where jihadis were routinely tortured and hanged] . . .

Osman called some days ago. He is fine but in intensive care [being monitored by the police]. When his situation improves he will call. He is considering looking for work with Salah al-Din [in Afghanistan], as opportunities are scarce where he is, but his health condition is the obstacle.

Though troubled by arrests abroad, the jihadis had time and safety for contemplation in Afghanistan. In 1999 al-Zawahiri undertook a top-secret program to develop chemical and biological weapons, a program he and others referred to on the computer as the "Yogurt" project. Though fearsome in its intent, the program had a proposed start-up budget of only $2,000 to $4,000. Fluent in English and French, al-Zawahiri began by studying foreign medical journals and provided summaries in Arabic for Muhammad Atef [former military commander of Al Qaeda], including the one that follows.

To: Muhammad Atef
From: Ayman al-Zawahiri

Folder: Outgoing Mail—To Muhammad Atef
Date: April 15, 1999

I have read the majority of the book [an unnamed volume,
probably on biological and chemical weapons] . . . [It] is
undoubtedly useful. It emphasizes a number of important facts,
such as:

a) *The enemy started thinking about these weapons before WWI.*
   Despite their extreme danger, we only became aware of them
   when the enemy drew our attention to them by repeatedly
   expressing concerns that they can be produced simply with
   easily available materials . . .

b) *The destructive power of these weapons is no less than that of*
   nuclear weapons.

c) *A germ attack is often detected days after it occurs, which*
   raises the number of victims.

d) *Defense against such weapons is very difficult, particularly if*
   large quantities are used . . .

   I would like to emphasize what we previously discussed—
that looking for a specialist is the fastest, safest, and cheapest
way [to embark on a biological- and chemical-weapons program].
Simultaneously, we should conduct a search on our own . . . Along
these lines, the book guided me to a number of references that I am
attaching. Perhaps you can find someone to obtain them . . .

The letter goes on to cite mid-twentieth-century articles from,
among other sources, *Science*, *The Journal of Immunology*, and
The New England Journal of Medicine, and lists the names of

such books as *Tomorrow's Weapons* (1964), *Peace or Pestilence* (1949), and *Chemical Warfare* (1921).

Al-Zawahiri and Atef appear to have settled on the development of a chemical weapon as the most feasible option available to them. Their exchanges on the computer show that they hired Medhat Mursi al-Sayed, an expert to whom they refer as Abu Khabab, to assist them. They also drew up rudimentary architectural plans for their laboratory and devised a scheme to create a charitable foundation to serve as a front for the operation. According to other sources, Abu Khabab gassed some stray dogs at a testing field in eastern Afghanistan, but there is no indication that al-Qaeda ever developed a chemical weapon it could deploy.

After 9/11

The first evidence of work on the computer following 9/11 comes just days after the attacks, in the form of a promotional video called "The Big Job"—a montage of television footage of the attacks and their chaotic aftermath, all set to rousing victory music. The office was surely busier than it had ever been before, and soon many members of al-Qaeda's inner circle were competing for time on the computer. Ramzi bin al-Shibh, the senior Yemeni operative who coordinated with Khalid Sheikh Muhammad in masterminding the attacks, used the computer to work on a hasty and unfinished ideological justification for the operation, which he titled "The Truth About the New Crusade: A Ruling on the Killing of Women and Children of the Non-Believers," excerpts of which follow:

Concerning the operations of the blessed Tuesday [9/11] . . . they are legally legitimate, because they are committed against a country at war with us, and the people in that country are combatants. Someone might say that it is the innocent, the elderly, the women, and the children who are victims, so how can these operations be legitimate according to sharia? And we say that the sanctity of women, children, and the elderly is not absolute. There are special cases . . . Muslims may respond in kind if infidels have targeted women and children and elderly Muslims, [or if] they are being invaded, [or if] the non-combatants are helping with the fight, whether in action, word, or any other type of assistance, [or if they] need to attack with heavy weapons, which do not differentiate between combatants and non-combatants . . .

Now that we know that the operations were permissible from the Islamic point of view, we must answer or respond to those who prohibit the operations from the point of view of benefits or harms . . .

There are benefits . . . The operations have brought about the largest economic crisis that America has ever known. Material losses amount to one trillion dollars. America has lost about two thousand economic brains as a result of the operations. The stock exchange dropped drastically, and American consumer spending deteriorated. The dollar has dropped, the airlines have been crippled, the American globalization system, which was going to spoil the world, is gone . . .

Because of Saddam and the Baath Party, America punished a whole population. Thus its bombs and its embargo killed millions of Iraqi Muslims. And because of Osama bin Laden, America surrounded Afghans and bombed them, causing the death of tens of thousands of Muslims . . .

God said to assault whoever assaults you, in a like manner.
. . . In killing Americans who are ordinarily off limits,
Muslims should not exceed four million non-combatants, or
render more than ten million of them homeless. We should
avoid this, to make sure the penalty [that we are inflicting] is
no more than reciprocal. God knows what is best.

Osama bin Laden himself was composing letters on the computer just weeks before the fall of Kabul. In them he defiantly
addressed the American people with a statement of al-Qaeda's
goals, which he then went on to spell out at much greater
length for Mullah Omar, in the spirit of a powerful, high-level
political adviser offering advice to a head of state.

To: The American People
From: Osama bin Laden
Folder: Publications
Date: October 3, 2001

What takes place in America today was caused by the flagrant inter-
ference on the part of successive American governments into others'
business. These governments imposed regimes that contradict the
faith, values, and lifestyles of the people. This is the truth that the
American government is trying to conceal from the American people.
*   Our current battle is against the Jews. Our faith tells us we*
shall defeat them, God willing. However, Muslims find that the
Americans stand as a protective shield and strong supporter, both
financially and morally. The desert storm that blew over New York
and Washington should, in our view, have blown over Tel Aviv.
The American position obliged Muslims to force the Americans out
of the arena first to enable them to focus on their Jewish enemy.

Why are the Americans fighting a battle on behalf of the Jews? Why do they sacrifice their sons and interests for them?

To: Mullah Omar
From: Osama bin Laden
Folder: Deleted File (Recovered)
Date: October 3, 2001

Highly esteemed Leader of the Faithful,
Mullah Muhammad Omar, Mujahid,
May God preserve him . . .

1. *We treasure your message, which confirms your generous, heroic position in defending Islam and in standing up to the symbols of infidelity of this time.*
2. *I would like to emphasize the major impact of your statements on the Islamic world. Nothing harms America more than receiving your strong response to its positions and statements. Thus it is very important that the Emirate respond to every threat or demand from America . . . with demands that America put an end to its support of Israel, and that U.S. forces withdraw from Saudi Arabia. Such responses nullify the effect of the American media on people's morale.*

    Newspapers mentioned that a recent survey showed that seven out of every ten Americans suffer psychological problems following the attacks on New York and Washington.

    Although you have already made strong declarations, we ask you to increase them to equal the opponent's media campaign in quantity and force.

    Their threat to invade Afghanistan should be countered by a threat on your part that America will not be able to dream of security until Muslims experience it as reality in Palestine and Afghanistan.

3. Keep in mind that America is currently facing two contradictory problems:

   a) If it refrains from responding to jihad operations, its prestige will collapse, thus forcing it to withdraw its troops abroad and restrict itself to U.S. internal affairs. This will transform it from a major power to a third-rate power, similar to Russia.

   b) On the other hand, a campaign against Afghanistan will impose great long-term economic burdens, leading to further economic collapse, which will force America, God willing, to resort to the former Soviet Union's only option: withdrawal from Afghanistan, disintegration, and contraction.

Thus our plan in the face of this campaign should focus on the following:

   — Serving a blow to the American economy, which will lead to:

   a) Further weakening of the American economy

   b) Shaking the confidence in the American economy. This will lead investors to refrain from investing in America or participating in American companies, thus accelerating the fall of the American economy . . .

   — Conduct a media campaign to fight the enemy's publicity. The campaign should focus on the following important points:

   a) Attempt to cause a rift between the American people and their government, by demonstrating the following to the Americans:

   —That the U.S. government will lead them into further losses of money and lives.

—*That the government is sacrificing the people to serve the interests of the rich, particularly the Jews.*
—*That the government is leading them to the war front to protect Israel and its security.*
—*America should withdraw from the current battle between Muslims and Jews.*

This plan aims to create pressure from the American people on their government to stop its campaign against Afghanistan, on the grounds that the campaign will cause major losses to the American people.
—*Imply that the campaign against Afghanistan will be responded to with revenge blows against America.*

I believe that we can issue, with your permission, a number of speeches that we expect will have the greatest impact, God willing, on the American, Pakistani, Arab, and Muslim people.

Finally, I would like to emphasize how much we appreciate the fact that you are our Emir. I would like to express our great appreciation of your historical stands in the service of Islam and in the defense of the Prophet's tradition. We ask God to accept and reward such stands.

We ask God to grant the Muslim Afghani nation, under your leadership, victory over the American infidels, just as He singled this nation out with the honor of defeating the Communist infidels.

We ask God to lead you to the good of both this life and the afterlife.

Peace upon you and God's mercy and blessings.
Your brother,
Osama Bin Muhammad Bin Laden

———◻———

The capture of Khalid Shaikh Mohammed (abbreviated throughout the following article as KSM) was an immense victory for the U.S. Federal Bureau of Investigation (FBI). The 9/11 Commission report named KSM the "principle architect of the 9/11 attacks." He has also been named responsible for organizing and financing several other terrorist atrocities including the 2002 nightclub bombing in Bali, the 1993 bombing of the World Trade Center, the 2000 bombing of the USS Cole, *and the murder of American journalist Daniel Pearl in 2002.*

Before his capture on March 1, 2003, KSM had been traveling under several passports, living luxuriously and making connections throughout the world. His arrest greatly damaged Al Qaeda's infrastructure and may have foiled a number of Al Qaeda plots in America. From days of heavy interrogation, the United States was able to gather vital information about plans to blow up the Brooklyn Bridge in New York City, and several gas stations throughout the country. **—AI**

"Al Qaeda in America: The Enemy Within"
by Evan Thomas
Newsweek, June 23, 2003

Khalid Shaikh Mohammed looked more like a loser in a T shirt than a modern-day Mephistopheles. But "KSM," as he is always referred to in FBI documents, held the key to unlock the biggest mystery of the war on terror: is Al Qaeda operating inside America?

The answer, according to KSM's confessions and the intense U.S. investigation that followed, is yes. It is not known where the authorities took KSM after he was captured, looking paunchy and pouty, in a 3 a.m. raid in Pakistan on March 1. As Al Qaeda's director of global operations, KSM was by far the most valuable prize yet captured by American intelligence and its various allies in the post-9-11 manhunt. He probably now resides in an exceedingly spartan jail cell in some friendly Arab country, perhaps Jordan.

He has probably not been tortured, at least in the traditional sense. Interrogation methods, usually involving sleep deprivation, have become much more refined. He probably did not tell all he knew. Qaeda chieftains are schooled in resisting interrogation, and informed sources said that at first KSM offered up nothing but evasions and disinformation. But confronted by the contents of his computer and his cell-phone records, he began speaking more truthfully. According to intelligence documents obtained by NEWSWEEK, many of the names, places, and plots he revealed have checked out. After 9-11, Osama bin Laden's terror network "was clearly here," a top U.S. law-enforcement official told NEWSWEEK. "It was organized, it was being directed by the leaders of Al Qaeda." Though rumors of sleeper cells have floated about for months, it is a startling revelation that Al Qaeda's chief of operations was directly running operatives inside the United States. Thanks to some real breakthroughs by the Feds, the Qaeda plots do not appear to have made it past the planning stage. The inside story of the war at home on Al Qaeda, reconstructed by NEWSWEEK reporters from intelligence documents and interviews with top officials, has been marked by good luck and good work. Still, no one in the intelligence community is declaring victory.

KSM revealed an overhaul of Al Qaeda's approach to penetrating America. The 9-11 hijackers were all foreign nationals—mostly Saudis, led by an Egyptian—who infiltrated the United States by obtaining student or tourist visas. To foil the heightened security after 9-11, Al Qaeda began to rely on operatives who would be harder to detect. They recruited U.S. citizens or people with legitimate Western passports who could move freely in the United States. They used women and family members as "support personnel." And they made an effort to find African-American Muslims who would be sympathetic to Islamic extremism. Using "mosques, prisons and universities throughout the United States," according to the documents, KSM reached deep into the heartland, lining up agents in Baltimore, Columbus, Ohio, and Peoria, Ill. The Feds have uncovered at least one KSM-run cell that could have done grave damage to the United States.

It is somewhat reassuring that, so far, at least, the FBI has not uncovered any plots to use chemical or biological or nuclear weapons against America. Al Qaeda chiefs, especially bin Laden's ghoulish No. 2, Ayman Al-Zawahiri, have shown a strong interest in the past in obtaining weapons of mass destruction. The terror network allegedly dispatched a Brooklyn-born Hispanic Catholic who converted to Islam, Jose Padilla, to scout out the possibility of building a radiological device, a so-called dirty bomb (arrested at Chicago's O'Hare airport in early 2002, he is being held as an "enemy combatant" in a military jail). But none of the operatives caught up in the web spun by KSM appears to have been working on a weapon that could wipe out an entire city.

On the other hand, the plotters were apparently scheming to take down the Brooklyn Bridge, destroy an airliner, derail a train and blow up a whole series of gas stations. Fortunately, American law enforcement has been able to nip these plots in the bud. The methods used by the G-men to crack the Qaeda cells, while effective and understandable under the circumstances, raise uncomfortable questions about legal means and ends.

Many of the Qaeda operatives have not been arrested or charged with a crime. The Bush Justice Department is reluctant to throw terror suspects into the American criminal-justice system, where they can avail themselves of lawyers and use their rights to tie prosecutors into knots (the alleged "20th hijacker" of the 9-11 plots, Zacarias Moussaoui, has succeeded in bringing his criminal prosecution to a grinding halt). Rather, the Justice Department has essentially been working in the shadows. FBI agents confronted some of the suspects directly and convinced them that it would be in their interest to work with the government without getting their own lawyers. Attorney General John Ashcroft recently told Congress that the Justice Department had obtained criminal plea agreements—"many under seal"—with more than 15 individuals who are cooperating with the government, leading to "critical intelligence" about Qaeda safe houses and recruiting tactics. But others—including some of those identified by KSM—may have been "turned" by the Feds. "You can't say they've been arrested," said one official. Some of the terror plotters confronted by the bureau have been secretly squirreled away in hotel rooms, living around the clock under FBI surveillance and working with the authorities to identify other Qaeda plots inside the country.

The cooperating witnesses have "given us a few leads" about "where to look," said one official, but, as yet, no major finds. That may be because Al Qaeda, like all successful terrorist organizations, is carefully "compartmented." Different cells are kept apart. Some top investigators have a nagging suspicion that KSM just fed his interrogators the small fry to divert investigators from the really big—and deadly—plots. "The problem is," said the senior official, "we don't know what we don't know."

Still, the Feds have learned a great deal more than the public record suggests. Ashcroft routinely gives lurid speeches about the enemy within. But the evidence from criminal prosecutions has been underwhelming. The Buffalo Six (later, Seven) rounded up as a terror cell looked more like some hapless, jobless American Muslims who had been lured into a Qaeda training camp on a pilgrimage to Pakistan. The threat level has bobbed back and forth between Yellow (Elevated) and Orange (High) four times in the last year. Alternately fearful and cynical, the public has become just plain weary.

But the "threat matrix" presented to President George W. Bush every morning at his daily intelligence briefing has been cause for genuine concern. As the Feds, working with foreign police, captured top-level Qaeda operatives after 9-11, interrogations and electronic eavesdropping revealed some scary plans. Abu Zubaydah, the Palestinian terrorist who ran Al Qaeda's training-camp network in Afghanistan, told interrogators that the bin Laden network was deeply interested in bringing down "the bridge in the Godzilla movie." That sci-fi fantasy led New York police to scramble to guard the Brooklyn Bridge every time there is a terror alert. Put under the hot lights, other Qaeda lieutenants named names and pointed to likely targets.

It was the seizure of Khalid Shaikh Mohammed in March that allowed the Feds to really begin to connect the dots. KSM is a fanatical and committed terrorist who has spent years planning the mass murder of Americans. Long before 9-11, he had planned (along with his nephew Ramzi Yousef, a plotter in the 1993 World Trade Center bombing) a fantastic exercise called Project Bojinka (Serbo-Croatian for "big bang") to blow up a dozen airliners over the Pacific Ocean. KSM's more recent pet project has been to disrupt the American economy by attacking its infrastructure. He wanted to destroy key transportation nodes—bridges, planes, trains and fuel supplies.

Indeed, KSM was planning to time some of these attacks, possibly against gas stations in New York and Washington, to coincide with the 9-11 attacks, but Osama bin Laden himself vetoed the idea, according to intelligence reports obtained by NEWSWEEK. Bin Laden was apparently worried about maintaining operational security for the spectacular hijackings. After 9-11, KSM revived the plans to attack a series of gas stations. According to Justice Department documents describing KSM's interrogation, he "tasked" a former resident of Baltimore named Majid Khan to "move forward" on Khan's plan to destroy several U.S. gas stations by "simultaneously detonating explosives in the stations' underground storage tanks." KSM was intimately involved in the details. When Khan reported that the storage tanks were unprotected and easy to attack, KSM wanted to be sure that explosive charges would cause a massive eruption of flame and destruction.

Khan—a "confessed AQ [Al Qaeda] member" who was apparently captured in Pakistan, according to intelligence sources—traveled at least briefly to the United States, where he tried unsuccessfully to seek asylum. His family members, intelligence documents say, are longtime Baltimore residents and own gas stations in that city (a detail NEWSWEEK was able to confirm). KSM told interrogators that he and Khan discussed a plan to use a Karachi-based import-export business to smuggle explosives into the United States.

Khan looked for more help from people who might escape the notice of investigators. KSM told interrogators that a woman named Aafia Siddiqui, a U.S. visa holder who has lived in the United States for a decade, rented a post-office box to help Khan establish his U.S. identity. Siddiqui was supposed to support "other AQ operatives as they entered the United States," according to the Feds' description of the plot. Siddiqui's estranged husband, identified by informed sources as Mohammad Amjan Khan, had purchased body armor, night-vision goggles and a variety of military manuals to send to Pakistan. He apparently returned these items after being interviewed by the FBI. Both Siddiqui and Khan were described as "medical professionals." Siddiqui fled to Pakistan, where she was reportedly arrested.

KSM told his interrogators that he wanted "two or three African-American Muslim converts" to carry out his operation to blow up the gas stations. Majid Khan told the FBI that he had seen "two African Americans (identified as such by their American accents) during a 2000 meeting in Pakistan with KSM and other AQ operatives."

KSM had more diabolical plans for another of Khan's American relatives, a commercial truckdriver named Iyman Faris (a.k.a. Mohammad Rauf). The truckdriver is a naturalized U.S. citizen, a longtime resident of Columbus, Ohio. His ex-wife told friends that in hindsight she finds it disturbing that her husband, a devout Muslim, had long expressed an interest in learning how to fly. He spent hours, she said, reading magazines about ultralight aircraft, gliders with small engines that can be piloted almost anywhere. The order to study ultralight aircraft came directly from KSM, according to intelligence documents.

The Qaeda operations chief told interrogators that he had a specific assignment for the truckdriver. He wanted Faris to case the Brooklyn Bridge. KSM also instructed Faris to obtain "gas cutters" (presumably, metal-cutting torches) that could be used to cut the Brooklyn Bridge's suspension wires. And more: the truckdriver was assigned to obtain "torque tools" to bend railroad tracks, the better to send a passenger train hurtling off the rails. And still more: Faris recommended driving a small truck with explosives beneath a commercial airliner as it sat on the tarmac. A licensed truckdriver, he said, could easily penetrate airport security.

None of these plots ever came off. Faris has disappeared. No one was home when NEWSWEEK knocked on the door of his apartment in a run-down section of Columbus last week. But as recently as last month, public records show, he paid a $200 fine and got his driver's license restored after being arrested for speeding in Delaware County. (His license recently expired, say Ohio state officials; he has not tried to renew it.)

Qaeda operatives seem to be dangerous drivers. Faris was busted for speeding in 1996 and for "failure to control his vehicle" in 1997, when he flipped his vehicle on a highway exit ramp, local officials say. An arrest for drunken driving marred the otherwise clean record of another suspected sleeper agent whose story is a chilling example of Al Qaeda's foothold in the American heartland.

During his interrogation, KSM identified a man named Ali S. Al-Marri as "the point of contact for AQ operatives arriving in the US for September 11 follow-on operations." KSM described Al-Marri as "the perfect sleeper agent because he has studied in the United States, had no criminal record, and had a family with whom he could travel." Actually, Al-Marri had been charged with driving under the influence in Peoria, Ill., in 1990. The Qatari national had returned to the United States on Sept. 10, 2001, to pick up a graduate degree in computer information systems from Peoria's Bradley University. He was accused by the FBI of phoning an alleged Qaeda operative in the United Arab Emirates, Qaeda paymaster Mustafa Ahmed al-Hawsawi, and lying about it that same December. Al-Marri's apartment was filled with Islamic jihadist materials. His computer included bookmarked Web sites for hazardous chemicals, computer hacking and fake IDs, according to court documents. Bookmarks in an almanac marked entries for dams, reservoirs and railroads. U.S. officials were outraged when the Saudi Embassy helped Al-Marri's wife obtain a passport to leave the United States in November (U.S. officials say she was still under subpoena; Saudi lawyers disagree). Al-Marri, who pleaded not guilty to charges of lying to investigators and credit-card fraud, is in prison in Peoria, awaiting trial.

Intelligence records obtained by NEWSWEEK list other Qaeda operatives who may be hiding out somewhere in America. "KSM has identified Adnan el Shukri Jumah, a Saudi born permanent US resident alien as an operative with standing permission to attack targets in the United States that had been previously approved by Usama bin Laden," reads one entry in a Homeland Security document. "El Shukri Jumah lived in the US for six years and received an associate's degree from a Florida college. He reportedly surveilled targets in New York, as well as the Panama Canal." Osama's made man has apparently vanished.

Intelligence officials say, however, that they are in some ways more worried about lone wolves who have only distant ties to Al Qaeda. "My concern is what we're seeing in the Gaza Strip and the West Bank," one top official told NEWSWEEK— the solo fanatic suicide bomber, or, in intelligence parlance, a "non-aligned mujahedin." These are the lost souls who wandered through Al Qaeda's Afghan training camps during the '90s and have gone on to create their own cells. They may pose a more imminent threat than the kind of top-of-the-line, well-trained operatives who carried out the complex, almost balletic 9-11 hijack plan.

Canada seems to be a haven for these folk. In late May, Canadian authorities finally moved to expel a pizza-parlor operator and Moroccan refugee named Adil Charkaoui under newly enacted provisions of an antiterrorist law. Charkaoui, who admits he traveled to Pakistan for "religious training," has long been tied to Ahmed Ressam, the alleged terrorist who was arrested as he entered the United States from Canada at the time of the 2000 Millennium celebrations. In his car were the makings of a bomb, which, he later confessed, was intended for an attack on the Los Angeles airport. Charkaoui, a martial-arts expert, has also been linked to the 9-11 plotters as well as to a plot to blow up an Air France jetliner.

American authorities fret that the Canadians allow sleepers to walk the streets until they are compelled to take legal action. Bush Justice Department officials have not been so reticent. By putting suspects in what one top law-enforcement official described to NEWSWEEK as "a kind of limbo detention"— essentially living with FBI agents who could charge them at any time—the Feds are pushing the legal envelope. "We're making this up as we go along," said the official. "It's a brave new world out there." When FBI agents confront Qaeda suspects, they give them a choice: cooperate or face the consequences, which could include a life in prison and possibly even the death penalty. (Justice Department spokeswoman Barbara Comstock declined to discuss any specific cases, but said that the department has deployed legal tactics that have been "historically used in organized crime and drug cases and proven effective in breaking down conspiracies.") One lever the Feds currently lack is the threat of expulsion from the United States. Some Bush administration officials would like to amend the law to allow prosecutors to strip terror suspects of their naturalized citizenship and deport them.

The FBI cannot hope to find every Qaeda operative, and certainly not every Islamic fanatic who wishes to conduct a jihad against America. Curiously, the best protection may be the soft power of daily life in the land of the free.

One intelligence official, wondering aloud why America has not been attacked since 9-11 despite the clear intentions of bin Laden's terror network, speculated that the sleeper agents just plain fall asleep. "A lot of these guys lose the jihadi, desert spirit," said the official. "They get families, they get jobs, and they lose the fire in the belly. Welcome to America."

———■———

When the United States, with assistance from British troops, invaded Afghanistan in October 2001, President Bush claimed that he would go after any nation that harbored terrorists, and asked the international community for support. However, after several civilian deaths in Afghanistan, many nations were uneasy about contributing to the campaign. A major concern was the impact the war might have on a nation that had already suffered through decades of poverty and strife. In addition, many nations expressed concern about whether the United States was ousting the Taliban from the region in the most efficient way, and whether the war would accomplish its goal of making the world a safer place.

Conscious of the lapse of worldwide support, the United States endeavored to win global approval of its invasion of Afghanistan while firmly maintaining its antiterrorism position and its intolerance of countries that harbored terrorists. The following New York Times *article reports on the various strategies used by the United States to increase worldwide support for war. —AI*

"U.S. Tries to Sway Worldwide Opinion in Favor of War"
by Michael R. Gordon
New York Times, November 6, 2001

The Bush administration, worried that public opinion abroad has turned against the American military campaign in Afghanistan, is making a major effort to take its case to the foreign—and especially the Islamic—news media.

On Tuesday, President Bush will give a speech about fighting terrorism, which will be beamed by satellite to a conference in Poland of Central European leaders. Top policy makers have also been making themselves available to the Islamic news media.

The administration's efforts to win international support for its campaign against Osama bin Laden's Qaeda network and the Taliban government in Afghanistan is inherently difficult because the message administration officials are providing at home is at odds with expectations of foreign governments.

While administration officials have sought to prepare Americans for a long and difficult conflict, Pakistan and other nations in the region are hoping for a short war and the quick exit of United States troops.

As part of the American information campaign, Gen. Richard B. Myers, chairman of the Joint Chiefs of Staff, recently gave an interview to Al Jazeera, the all-news Arab satellite television channel that broadcast Mr. bin Laden's tirades against the United States. Today, Secretary of State Colin L. Powell gave an interview to Egyptian television.

The State Department is also planning a television and advertising campaign to try to influence Islamic opinion; one segment could feature American celebrities, including sports stars, and a more emotional message. It is being planned by Charlotte Beers, the new undersecretary of state for public diplomacy, who came to the administration after a long career on Madison Avenue.

In all conflicts, winning the information war has been an essential element of military strategy. But with lingering resentment in the Arab world about America's superpower status, support for Israel and cultural dominance, countering the Taliban's information offensive has not been easy.

The United States says its intense air attacks are necessary to destroy the terrorist network and topple the Taliban government, and it has stressed that it is trying to avoid civilian casualties and is not at war with the Afghan people. But the specter of bombs falling on an impoverished country that has been ravaged by war for more than two decades has been used by the Taliban to foment opposition to Americans.

Public sentiment in Islamic countries could have profound implications for American national security. An upheaval in Pakistan, for example, could raise concerns about the security of its nuclear stockpile. It could also deprive the United States of a base of operations for its military campaign. The American military is also using bases in the Persian Gulf.

"We have been hearing from Arab leaders and others who support us who say you guys need to do more," a senior administration official said, referring to the information campaign. "They say, 'Al Jazeera is killing us.'"

One nation where the message conveyed in the American media has provoked anger is Saudi Arabia, where Crown Prince Abdullah criticized reports questioning the kingdom's commitment to the anti-terrorism effort. In a speech broadcast Sunday he said President Bush, in a recent telephone call, had expressed regrets for stories that drove a wedge between the countries.

The White House today did not characterize the comments as an apology, saying the president believed that any depiction of the United States at odds with Saudi Arabia was wrong.

The Islamic world, however, is not the only concern for Washington. Reports that civilians have been bombed have led to a measurable drop in European support for the campaign. "The conduct of the war alarms Europe," the French newspaper *Le Monde* said recently.

To soothe Islamic opinion, the Pentagon has modulated the message it has delivered in the region. Defense Secretary Donald H. Rumsfeld said today that the war might be over in a matter of months.

"Do I think Afghanistan will take years?" he said at a news conference in India. "No, I don't."

In a Pentagon briefing last week, however, Mr. Rumsfeld sent a different message to the American people. "We're still in the very, very early stages of this conflict," he said. "The U.S. bombed Japan for three and a half years, until August 1945, before they accomplished their objectives."

To influence international public opinion, the United States and Britain are also establishing information centers in Washington, London and Pakistan to field questions about the war.

Even senior administration officials concede that the White House was slow to realize the power of Al Jazeera as a channel to the Arab world, and that it lost valuable time in the early days of the war by not pushing its message to the satellite channel.

That has changed. Condoleezza Rice, the national security adviser, Mr. Rumsfeld, General Myers and Secretary Powell have all given interviews to Al Jazeera. Secretary Powell also recently gave an interview to *Al Hayat*, an Arabic-language newspaper in London. Senior State Department officials also speak regularly by video conference call with Arab journalists based in London.

But those interviews are set-piece exercises. An important tactical shift occurred on Saturday after the administration learned that Mr. bin Laden had made another tape available to Al Jazeera.

Ari Fleischer, the White House spokesman, said today that the administration quickly arranged for Christopher Ross, a former American ambassador to Syria who is fluent in Arabic, to go on Al Jazeera and read a statement in response.

Even so, the administration has struggled with finding Arab and non-Arab Islamic allies to speak to the region on America's behalf.

"This is a war against terror, and not against Islam," a senior military officer said. "We need to have Islamic voices saying that."

To that end, Mr. Fleischer today trumpeted comments from Amr Moussa, the secretary general of the Arab League, who said Mr. bin Laden did not act of behalf of Muslims.

For all of its public relations efforts, however, the administration is involved in an uphill battle with much of Islamic public opinion, including opinion inside Afghanistan.

Today the Voice of America began broadcasts into Afghanistan citing seventh-century battles by the Prophet Muhammad to argue that Islamic armies have conducted attacks during Ramadan.

"As President George W. Bush put it," the broadcast said, "the enemy won't rest during Ramadan, and neither will we."

———◻———

On March 19, 2003, the United States invaded Iraq. The justification for the invasion was twofold: 1) Iraq had access to weapons of mass destruction (WMDs) and thus was a threat to the United States and other countries, and 2) Iraq's leader Saddam Hussein had developed a relationship with Al Qaeda that threatened U.S. security. However, in July 2004, the 9/11 Commission made a statement that there wasn't any evidence that Iraq and Al Qaeda had developed a relationship.

Clearly, something was amiss. One group, the president of the United States and his advisers, claimed that Al Qaeda and Saddam Hussein had established a relationship and were working together to plan attacks on the United States. The other party, the 9/11 Commission, said the opposite: that Saddam Hussein and Al Qaeda were not conspiring to harm the United States.

*In the following article, journalist David Corn
offers his opinion on the debate over the alleged connection between Al Qaeda and Saddam Hussein. —AI*

"Al Qaeda Disconnect"
by David Corn
The Nation, July 5, 2004

"The connection"—neoconservative shorthand for the pur-
ported link between Saddam Hussein and Al Qaeda—is
crumbling. Two days after Vice President Cheney asserted that
Saddam "had long-established ties with Al Qaeda" and one day
after George W. Bush echoed his second-in-command, the independent bipartisan 9/11 commission said that no such bond
existed. In a staff statement the commission notes, "There
have been reports that contacts between Iraq and al Qaeda . . .
occurred after Bin Ladin had returned to Afghanistan [in
1996], but they do not appear to have resulted in a collabora-
tive relationship." According to the commission, bin Laden
"explored possible cooperation with Iraq" in the early 1990s
("despite his opposition to Hussein's secular regime"), a senior
Iraqi intelligence officer met bin Laden in 1994 and bin Laden
asked Iraq for space where he could establish training camps
and for assistance in obtaining weapons. But, the commission
concludes, "Iraq apparently never responded." Regarding possible Iraqi involvement in the 9/11 plot, the commission
states, "We have no credible evidence that Iraq and al Qaeda
cooperated on attacks against the United States."

With one paragraph, the commission decimates a primary
rationale of Bush's war on Iraq. Before the invasion, Bush

argued that Saddam was an immediate threat and war was necessary because (a) Iraq possessed weapons of mass destruction, and (b) Saddam was in cahoots with Al Qaeda and at any moment could slip bin Laden WMDs to use against the United States. As Bush proclaimed in November 2002, Saddam was "a threat because he is dealing with Al Qaeda." But he produced no proof then, and, according to the commission, he has none now.

There were contacts between Al Qaeda and Iraq, but it appears that a relationship never blossomed. The 9/11 report, however, does indicate that there were several nations essential to Al Qaeda's growth and development. Sudan supported it extensively in the early 1990s. Bin Laden's operatives obtained training in explosives, intelligence and security from Iran. Pakistan "facilitated" the "Taliban's ability to provide Bin Ladin a haven." The governments of Pakistan and Iran apparently permitted recruits to transit their nations to bin Laden's training camps (perhaps 20,000 jihadis overall flocked to these facilities). Saudi Arabia was "fertile fundraising ground" for Al Qaeda, which depended on informal money-transfer networks in Pakistan and the United Arab Emirates. In fact, it seems that Al Qaeda could not have thrived without official or unofficial assistance in many countries. But according to the commission, Iraq was not among them.

Before and after the Iraq invasion, Cheney and others tried to tie Saddam to the 9/11 attacks. Asked this past September if Saddam had anything to do with 9/11, Cheney again referred to the allegation that Mohamed Atta, lead 9/11 plotter, had met with a senior Iraqi intelligence officer in Prague five months before the strikes. Cheney was not reluctant about pushing this charge, although the CIA and FBI had already concluded that it was probably untrue. And in recent weeks neocon hawks like former CIA chief R. James Woolsey have continued to blow on the embers of the Atta-in-Prague story. But in another staff statement, the 9/11 commission declares, "Based on the evidence available—including investigation by Czech and U.S. authorities plus detainee reporting—we do not believe that such a meeting occurred."

But "the connection" persists—at least for Bush. The day before the 9/11 commission released these reports, a reporter asked Bush to provide "the best evidence" for claiming that Saddam was in league with Al Qaeda. "Zarqawi is the best evidence," Bush said. "Remember the e-mail exchange between Al Qaeda and he, himself, about how to disrupt the progress toward freedom" in Iraq? This reference was to Abu Musab al-Zarqawi, a terrorist operating in Iraq. Earlier this year, the Kurds intercepted a letter (not an e-mail) Zarqawi supposedly sent to Al Qaeda asking for help fomenting civil war in Iraq. According to US officials, Al Qaeda turned down the request. This exchange, if it indicates anything, is evidence of a division between the two terrorist camps. And Zarqawi has been linked in the past not to Saddam's regime but to Ansar al-Islam, a terrorist outfit that declared its opposition to Saddam.

If Zarqawi was the best evidence Bush could offer, he had a paltry case for going to war. Moreover, the 9/11 commission's findings show that Bush and the entire "connection" crowd were—and remain—disconnected from the known facts.

———■———

Andrew C. McCarthy, a senior fellow at the Foundation for the Defense of Democracies, describes the response of the U.S. government in the years following 9/11 as "a stunning achievement." As evidence he offers President George W. Bush's reelection in 2004, and the fact that since 9/11 the United States has not suffered a major terrorist attack.

McCarthy credits the government's success in preventing recent terrorist attacks as a "result of getting serious." Most notable, he commends the Bush administration for its policy of aggressively pursuing terrorists and enemies of America in Afghanistan and Iraq. He also lauds the passing of the post-9/11 Patriot Act, and even 1996 legislation by the Clinton administration that revamped antiterror law in the United States. —AI

"Three Years and Counting"
by Andrew C. McCarthy
National Review, December 13, 2004

The September 11 attacks still reverberate profoundly. Of that, there is no better indication than George W. Bush's decisive reelection. For all the trendy talk about "values voters," the campaign was run principally on national-security issues, and the president won a surprisingly large majority. The nation was convinced that he had a superior handle on how to keep us safe.

And there's a reason for that conviction: In the three years since 9/11 and the still-unsolved anthrax scare that followed hard on it, the U.S. has not suffered a domestic terrorist attack. One might ask: Is that truly attributable to President Bush's stewardship? After all, we are continually told that

Islamist militants are gifted with preternatural reservoirs of patience; could it not be that we are simply in another cyclical downturn, a calm before the next inevitable storm?

Not a chance. The failure of al-Qaeda, its affiliates, and assorted Wahhabi wannabes to strike us when we have every indication they are desperately trying to is a direct result of the Bush doctrine, announced and implemented in the aftermath of 9/11. The president, the Pentagon, and the Justice Department are to be commended for persevering in it despite a relentless barrage of criticism from the media, civil-liberties extremists, and, regrettably, too many Democrats. Especially salient on this score have been two aspects of the doctrine: a comprehensive strategy that brings to bear all of government's arsenal, and the admonition to state sponsors that they will be considered just as culpable, and will be treated with the same lethality, as the terrorists they abet. Most of all, however, success has been the result of getting serious.

The holistic approach to terrorism has a number of advantages so palpable that the more interesting question is why it took a cataclysm of 9/11 dimensions to get it implemented. Most obviously, our military has killed or captured thousands of militants overseas. Incapacitated terrorists don't commit attacks. This is not a trite observation. First, unlike sovereigns, sub-state terror groups have extremely limited resources. To be sure, lost terrorists can be replaced in numerical terms—and are being replaced owing to prodigious funding streams globally backing madrassas that churn out an alarming number of terrorists-in-waiting. But instantly replacing the deadly competence of experienced hands is impossible. Second, the pantheon of jihadists who have become household names over the last few years—bin Laden, Zarqawi, Zawahiri, Khalid Sheik Mohammed, Sheik Omar Abdel Rahman (the blind sheik), Ramzi Yousef, and others—do not strike once and retire. Motivated by hatred and depravity masquerading as spirituality, they are even more likely to be recidivists than ordinary criminals. Neutralizing them does not prevent just one atrocity—it nullifies many.

On par with targeting the sheer number of terrorists has been addressing their motivation. Prosecution in the criminal-justice system was virtually the exclusive American response to terrorism from the time of the infamous "Black Hawk Down" debacle in Somalia in early 1993—after which the U.S. became resolutely casualty-averse—through October 2001, when President Bush dispatched the military to crush al-Qaeda and the Taliban in Afghanistan. The result? Although the nation was attacked repeatedly in that eight-year interim, fewer than three dozen terrorists were convicted in federal court—and those at a cost of unknown millions. Eliminating such a piddling fraction of a committed enemy at a time when its ranks were swelling into the tens of thousands was a sure prescription to be hit repeatedly. Nothing galvanizes an opposition, nothing spurs its recruiting, like the killer combination of successful attacks and a conceit that the adversary is pusillanimous. For zealots willing to immolate themselves in suicide-bombing and hijacking operations, mere prosecution is a provocatively weak response.

Similarly, appeasement is an invitation to more barbarity. Yet, as Norman Podhoretz detailed in an important essay ("World War IV") in the September issue of *Commentary*, it was a consistent element of U.S. counterterrorism policy in the quarter-century before 9/11. Indeed, the Reagan administration's disastrous pullout from Lebanon in 1983 after a barracks bombing by Hezbollah killed nearly 250 Marines is still a standard talking point for bin Laden and other jihadists—who bray to recruits that Americans give in when the body count gets high enough.

President Bush has now bulldozed that image. By making clear that his intention is not merely to contain but to eradicate international terror networks that threaten the U.S.; by indicating that terrorism is essentially a military challenge, as to which law enforcement plays an important but decidedly subordinate role; and by following through with formidable force in Afghanistan and Iraq, he has not merely decimated the enemy's numbers and its capacity to project power. He has also dramatically altered the enemy's perception of America as a nation to be trifled, rather than reckoned, with. Even those who despise us were guaranteed to become more tepid once it was certain that a swift and devastating response would be the price of a strike.

This assurance has had an underappreciated effect on state sponsors. Yes, al-Qaeda is a serious enemy . . . for a terrorist organization. But it is not a nation. It has no navy, it has no air force, and it has (at least we currently believe) neither ballistic missiles capable of striking the U.S. nor the types of payloads that can make such weapons an existential threat. To be a credible enemy, even the most professional terrorist network needs help from sovereign powers. Without such help, mounting an attack—while far from impossible—becomes much more difficult. The U.S., once again, becomes a tough target because of the natural advantages of geography and resources that made us a world power in the 19th century, before the age of air forces, submarines, and ICBMs seemed to make those advantages passé.

Striking the Rogue States

It has been popular in the past ten years or so for theorists to wax eloquent about a post-sovereign world in which the major threats come from sub-national entities. But this view dramatically underestimates the key role still played, and advantages still enjoyed, by modern states. Only countries have borders that are protected from attack by international law; have personnel that operate in other countries—even unfriendly countries—under the cover of diplomatic immunity; have the capacity to collect and disseminate sensitive intelligence (among other things) with impunity via diplomatic pouch; have the authority to issue travel documents that facilitate international movement; have the ability to tax people to support their agendas; and have military entities privileged to conduct training and weapons production (and, as we've seen in Iran, North Korea, Pakistan, Libya, and elsewhere, able as a practical matter to develop weapons of mass destruction).

At its most potent, al-Qaeda basked in state support. Sudan, Afghanistan, and, later, Iran gave it safe haven for command and control, training, and recruitment; and, as Clinton counterterrorism coordinator Richard Clarke asserted in the late 1990s, Iraq also offered bin Laden a soft place to land. The war we are currently fighting should have begun after our East African embassies were attacked in August 1998, and certainly no later than the USS *Cole* bombing in October 2000. But President Clinton declined to apply his considerable

skills to unwinding al-Qaeda's sovereign safety net, which
included not only its Taliban hosts but their allies in Pakistan
(which freely allowed its borders to be crossed for terrorist
recruitment and training purposes, and whose intelligence
service was compromised in bin Laden's cause). Al-Qaeda
enjoyed a steady influx of precious funding that would have
been impossible without countenance, if not outright complic-
ity, on the part of Saudi Arabia, the United Arab Emirates, and
other bastions of Sunni dominance. Bin Laden, moreover,
received weapons development assistance from Iraq, as well
as from Iran and Syria through Hezbollah.

None of this was a mystery to U.S. intelligence. Indeed,
some of it was publicly charged in indictments filed against
various terrorists. The Clinton administration, however, subor-
dinated these concerns to other priorities—the desire to be
seen as an honest broker rather than an Israeli ally in the so-
called "peace process," the elevation of challenging Pakistan
on nuclear proliferation over cultivating it on counterterrorism,
the fear of creating instability and resentment in the Muslim
world, etc. The Bush doctrine has changed all that. This doesn't
mean the problems the Clinton administration grappled with
were not real ones; they clearly were. Now, though, other
nations are on notice that the U.S. regards ending state support of terror networks that threaten America as its most
urgent policy imperative, and that we are willing to risk setbacks in other areas to promote national security.

The effect has been startling. Nations that once coddled
al-Qaeda are now American allies, or at least feel the need to
demonstrate concretely that they have ceased to support bin
Laden. Without such support, al-Qaeda is a shell of its former

self, and the remnants of its upper echelon have to spend their waking hours on how to survive until tomorrow, rather than on scripting tomorrow's attack. The nature of bin Laden's organization has thus undergone a radical change. It is still a threat, but an atomized one. There are cells throughout the world, but the command structure is decimated, and the cells—staffed with less experienced recruits—are not as capable as the halcyon al-Qaeda of the late 1990s.

This development plays strongly to our advantage: Cells operate best when they can blend into the community at large, and it is therefore not surprising that bin Laden's greatest achievements prior to 9/11 occurred in places like Mogadishu, Nairobi, Dar es Salaam, and Aden—Islamic cities with pockets of ardent militant sympathizers. Such places do not exist on the same scale inside the U.S. While 9/11 was a spectacular terrorist success, it has not altered the reality that it is not an easy proposition for a guerrilla faction without a navy or air force to attack American territory. The 1993 World Trade Center bombing took over a year to plan, and the laborious bomb-building (involving numerous meetings, other communications, renting safehouses, purchasing and transporting chemicals, etc.) took months. With law enforcement and public awareness now at unprecedented heights, it is an extreme challenge for militants in a vastly non-Muslim country to go undetected through the exertions required for a major attack.

That could all change if we lost our resolve. We are unlikely to, however, because of three developments. First, under the direction of attorney general John Ashcroft and FBI director Robert Mueller, the Justice Department and FBI have undergone a seismic culture shift. Their philosophy is now prevention first and prosecution second; they are more focused on stopping the next attack than on securing indictments after innocents have been slaughtered.

The other two changes have to do with the good and the bad of the Clinton years. As for the good, President Clinton and his Justice Department deserve enormous credit for revamping antiterror law in 1996. Prior to that time, the bias in the federal penal code was toward prosecuting completed acts of mass murder. The 1996 legislation significantly modified the law, placing desperately needed emphasis on the preparatory phases—by, among other things, criminalizing the provision of material support to terrorism; geometrically increasing the penalties for conspiracies, attempts, and threats to commit terrorist acts; and making it far easier for the Treasury Department to choke funding channels. To the limited extent the post-9/11 Patriot Act affected these areas, it was merely to refine what was already in place.

Unfortunately, much of the good done on the prosecution side was undermined by the Clinton Justice Department on the investigative side, including, most perilously, the needless heightening of the so-called wall that prevented intelligence agents and criminal investigators from pooling information to—as the numbingly repeated phrase goes—"connect the dots." While it is very unlikely investigators could have prevented 9/11, with such an impediment in place they never really had a chance.

The Patriot Act's dismantling of the wall is a signal achievement, and the Justice Department rightly credits it with several convictions rung up on conspiracy and material-support charges in the last three years. These prosecutions, necessarily involving nascent plots and ambiguous threats, have occasionally been belittled as overkill in the mainstream press, which bizarrely compares them unfavorably with the sensational terror prosecutions of the 1990s. But, of course, those cases seemed weightier because they usually followed murderous terror attacks. If we are to continue to avoid attack, less flashy enforcement—focusing on preparatory crimes, money laundering, immigration violations, and the like—must be the wave of the future. The prevention-first philosophy also means maintaining other Patriot Act improvements that sensibly gave agents conducting intelligence investigations the same evidence-gathering tools long available to criminal investigators. These tools, many of which—like repeal of the wall—will sunset at the end of 2005 if not extended by Congress, have made it feasible to strangle domestic terror threats in the cradle.

Three-plus years without an attack is not itself insurance against future threats, but neither is it an accident. It is the direct result of a national-security strategy that takes the battle forcibly to the enemy overseas, strenuously discourages other countries from providing terror networks with urgently needed support, and, domestically, makes prevention and diligence paramount over post-attack prosecution. It is a stunning achievement.

CHAPTER FIVE

GLOBAL CONNECTIONS: AL QAEDA AND THE WORLD

One day, one month, and one year after 9/11, terrorists bombed a nightclub in Bali, an island that is part of Indonesia. The attack, the bloodiest Indonesia had ever seen, claimed the lives of more than 200 people and left several hundred more wounded. The majority of the victims were foreign tourists.

Jemaah Islamiah, a radical Islamic group and the prime suspect behind the attacks, has long been suspected by several intelligence agencies of being in cahoots with Al Qaeda. After the Bali bombing, Jemaah Islamiah's leader, Abubakar Ba'asyir, was found guilty of conspiracy and was sentenced to two and a half years in prison. The group has also been accused of several other bombings in Asia, such as a series of bombings in Manila, the Philippines; and the bombing of the Australian Embassy in Jakarta, Indonesia, in 2004. The group has been believed to be instrumental in the spread of Al Qaeda's doctrine and recruitment in Southeast Asia.

The following article examines why Indonesia has become fertile ground for Al Qaeda activity and the government's response to ensure that attacks like the Bali bombing don't happen again. —AI

"Al-Qaeda's New Proving Ground"
by Romesh Ratnesar
Time, October 28, 2002

Until the moment their world came apart on Oct. 12, the surfers and club kids who flocked to the idyllic resort of Bali had little reason to believe they were in any particular danger. The U.S. had issued a general travel advisory about increased al-Qaeda activity around the globe. But the possibility that terrorists would strike Bali, a Hindu island in mostly Muslim Indonesia, seemed so remote that several officials from the U.S. embassy in Jakarta decided to spend their Columbus Day weekend there; one of them was relaxing just outside the Sari Club an hour before it blew up.

The scale, deadliness and timing of the Bali bombings were unanticipated, but they did not come as a complete shock to U.S. counterterrorism authorities. U.S. intelligence sources told TIME that in several meetings with Indonesian President Megawati Sukarnoputri since early September, Administration officials have informed her that the U.S. had evidence that al-Qaeda had established a major presence in Indonesia. They pressed her to arrest Islamic militants they believed were linked to Osama bin Laden's network, including Abubakar Ba'asyir, the alleged spiritual leader of Jemaah Islamiah, a radical Islamic group suspected of terrorist attacks across the region. Two days before the bombings, U.S. Ambassador Ralph Boyce told Megawati that if she did not begin cracking down, the U.S. would close its embassy, which might drain Indonesia of American investment and devastate its economy. "We put it to them very hard," says a senior State Department official.

It took one awful night in Bali for the message to get through. The Megawati government last week acknowledged that al-Qaeda is active on Indonesian soil, granted intelligence authorities the power to interrogate suspected terrorists without proof of wrongdoing and finally placed Ba'asyir under arrest. But the Bali attacks suggest it may be too late to prevent al-Qaeda from making the vast Indonesian archipelago a new sanctuary. "We've been talking with them for a long time about the seriousness of the problem," Deputy Secretary of Defense Paul Wolfowitz, a former ambassador to Indonesia, told TIME. "There's obviously a lot more to do, and maybe this will serve as a wake-up call for them."

Though the vast majority of Indonesians practice a moderate form of Islam, the country is an attractive haven for Muslim extremists. Monitoring terrorist activity in a swath of territory that spans more than 13,000 islands would test the mettle of any government, let alone a democracy as young and fractious as Indonesia's. Since the start of her tenure last year Megawati has shied away from trying to snuff out the extremist threat, in part to placate religious conservatives like Vice President Hamzah Haz, Megawati's likely opponent in the 2004 presidential race, who has long supported radical groups and has denied that there are any terrorists in Indonesia.

Haz was chosen by parliament to replace Megawati as Vice President after she was elected by the same body to succeed the impeached Abdurrahman Wahid. Haz is the head of Indonesia's main Muslim political group, the United Development Party, the third largest party in parliament; in 1999 he opposed Megawati's first bid for the presidency on the ground that the world's largest Muslim country should not be run by a woman. Megawati's secular Indonesian Democratic Party of Struggle controls just one-third of the seats in parliament. High unemployment and chronic government corruption have caused many to doubt her resolve to tackle tough problems. So to hang on to power and get re-elected in 2004, Megawati can't afford to ignore the conservatives. "Every politician in Indonesia needs the Islamic vote, and with Megawati it's even more so because of her secular nationalist background," says Arbi Sanit, a lecturer in politics at the University of Indonesia.

Efforts to get tough on terrorism are complicated by the government's desire to keep its distance from the military and security services, which were notoriously abusive under long-time dictator Suharto. A Western diplomat in Jakarta says if Megawati were to hand law-enforcement authorities too much power, "moderates of all stripes would make common cause against her out of fear that it marked the beginning of a return to the draconian methods of the Suharto days." Says Wolfowitz: "Americans need to understand we're dealing with a country that only recently became free after 50 years of dictatorship. Indonesians are leery about giving too much authority to the police." Whatever the causes, says Rohan Gunaratna, an expert on al-Qaeda at St. Andrews University in Scotland, Indonesia is "the only place in the world" where radicals linked to bin Laden "aren't being hunted down."

Last month the U.S. began ratcheting up the pressure on Indonesia. In early September, Omar al-Faruq, a senior al-Qaeda operative arrested in Bogor, Indonesia, in June, confessed to U.S. investigators his involvement in a string of planned terrorist attacks in the region. According to a CIA account of the interview, first disclosed by TIME last month, al-Faruq said Jemaah Islamiah's Ba'asyir had conspired in several of the plots and had ordered his followers to cooperate with al-Qaeda. (Ba'asyir has long denied any connection to terrorism, and is suing TIME over its report.) In mid-September, after phoning Megawati to discuss the threats detailed by al-Faruq, President Bush sent National Security Council aide Karen Brooks to Jakarta to press the Indonesians for action. On Sept. 23, after a grenade exploded near the Jakarta residence of an American embassy worker, U.S. officials told Indonesian counterparts they feared that the al-Qaeda threat "was changing form and going after softer targets"—such as sites frequented by tourists, according to a senior U.S. official.

After a tearful visit to the bombing site in Bali, Megawati soon displayed a newfound steeliness, rushing through an emergency presidential decree mandating tough antiterrorism regulations. Indonesian police ordered Ba'asyir to appear for questioning not in connection with the Bali attacks but for a spate of church bombings in 2000. But first, after giving a news conference in which he said "the Americans and Jews are terrorists," Ba'asyir collapsed and was hospitalized; the next day Indonesian police put him under arrest in the hospital. Signing on at last to the war on terrorism could cost Megawati support from Islamic hard-liners—or worse, incite violence from Ba'asyir's followers, who had promised to revolt if their leader were arrested. Though radical groups make up a tiny minority of the population, there is the possibility that they could further undermine the authority of the central government, making Indonesia even more hospitable to terrorists. "Al-Qaeda is already here and capable of launching more attacks," says a Western diplomat in Jakarta. "It's obvious there don't have to be many of them to do damage."

———◼———

On March 11, 2004, 200 people were killed and 1,500 wounded in a series of train bombings in Madrid, Spain, during the morning rush hour. It was the largest civilian attack in Europe since World War II. The act was initially credited to the ETA (Euskadi Ta Askatasuna, or Basque Homeland and Liberty), a terrorist organization that seeks an independent state for the Basque people. However, upon the discovery of further evidence—namely a recovered letter and videotape—the bombings were linked to an Islamist terrorist group that may have ties to Al Qaeda. Widespread conjecture supposed the subway bombings were a reaction to Spain's involvement in the Iraq war.

The bombings were politically significant for many reasons, but perhaps most important because they occurred three days before the Spanish general elections. Jose Maria Aznar, who had supported the Bush administration and had sent Spanish troops to Iraq, was succeeded as prime minister by Jose Luis Rodriguez Zapatero from the Socialist Party. This result was expected to significantly alter Spanish politics and foreign policy, especially concerning Spain's relationship with the United States. —AI

"Following Attacks, Spain's Governing Party Is Beaten"
by Elaine Sciolino
New York Times, March 15, 2004

Spain's opposition Socialists swept to an upset victory in general elections on Sunday, ousting the center-right party of Prime Minister Jose Maria Aznar in a groundswell of voter anger and grief over his handling of terrorist bombings in Madrid last week.

Investigators reported Sunday that there was growing evidence of involvement of Muslim fundamentalists in the attacks. They said one of five men arrested in the bombings had been linked to a suspected cell of Al Qaeda in Spain, and a Spanish antiterrorism official said several of the men had been under surveillance before the attacks.

The bombings, the deadliest terror attack in Europe since World War II, turned on its head what just a few days ago seemed to be a likely victory by Mr. Aznar's Popular Party. Some voters apparently believed that Al Qaeda had plotted the attacks to punish Mr. Aznar for supporting the war, which Spaniards overwhelmingly opposed.

With each new bit of information about the investigation into the attack came accusations that Mr. Aznar's party may have tried to suppress evidence of possible Al Qaeda involvement by assuming that Basque separatists were responsible.

In addition to the men who have been arrested, the Spanish authorities were investigating the possible involvement in the plot of other militant Muslims previously known to Spanish intelligence officials.

One official said investigators were examining how militants active in Spain may have joined with others from abroad to carry out the attack.

The threat of terrorism became more of a reality to many in Europe. In Germany, the government held an emergency meeting of its security cabinet. Interior Minister Otto Schily said Germany was asking for an emergency gathering of European police and security officials to form what he called a "common assessment" of the terrorism danger and to "coordinate how to respond."

The Socialist victory in Spain was seen as a repudiation of Mr. Aznar, whose party has been in office for eight years, and his close bonds with President Bush. It also posed a new problem for the American-led occupation force in Iraq, where Spain has 1,300 troops, because the Socialists have said they will withdraw them in the absence of a clear United Nations mandate.

Rage at the government overshadowed Election Day. Protesters shouted "Liar!" and "Get our troops out of Iraq!" at the Popular Party candidate Mariano Rajoy, the 48-year-old lawyer who had been expected to be Mr. Aznar's successor, as he voted at a Madrid polling station.

Jose Luis Rodriguez Zapatero, the 43-year-old lawyer who will become prime minister, accepted victory at his party's campaign headquarters by asking for a moment of silence for the bombing victims.

He called for "restrained euphoria" in light of the bombings, which killed 200 people and wounded 1,500 on four commuter trains in Madrid on Thursday.

"Terror should know that it has all of us in front of it and we will conquer it," he said. "I will lead a quiet change. I will govern for all in unity. And power will not change me, I promise you that."

In his speech conceding defeat, Mr. Rajoy praised Mr. Zapatero as a "worthy opponent" and pledged that the Popular Party would be "a loyal opposition always serving the interests of Spain."

But Mr. Rajoy noted that the election had been "inexorably marked by the atrocious attack" of terrorism. Mr. Aznar, who had hand-picked Mr. Rajoy as his successor, stood solemnly at his side.

The arrest of three Moroccans and two Indians and an official announcement, just hours before the polls opened, of a videotape in which a man claimed that Al Qaeda had carried out the bombings prompted accusations that the government was lying when it claimed that the violent Basque separatist movement ETA was most likely responsible.

In November, Mr. Zapatero called for the withdrawal of Spanish troops from Iraq after the death of seven Spanish secret service agents in an ambush. More recently, he softened his position, saying that if he won the election, he would withdraw the troops at the end of June unless a United Nations–led force took charge.

He also said during the campaign that Mr. Aznar's government had slavishly followed the United States, deepened European divisions over the war and damaged Spain's relationship with France and Germany.

The governing party "has gambled everything on its blind support for the United States, or rather the Bush administration, at the price of weakening the bond between Spain and Europe," he said in January.

According to official election figures, the Socialists won 43 percent of the vote and 164 seats in the 350-member Chamber of Deputies; the Popular Party won 38 percent of the vote and 148 seats.

Both the Popular Party and the biggest left-wing party, United Left, lost support to the Socialists. In 2000, the Popular Party won 183 seats, compared with 125 for the Socialists.

The Socialists were short of the 176 seats to have a majority necessary to form a government, which means it must create a coalition with another party or parties.

Mr. Aznar will remain the head of government until a new government is formed, which, under complicated electoral rules and the Constitution, could take about three months.

The turnout was higher than expected. More than 77 percent of the country's 35 million eligible voters cast ballots, compared with 55 percent four years ago. In Madrid, the figure was 80 percent.

In a television appearance on Saturday night, Mr. Rajoy alienated some voters when he called spontaneous antigovernment rallies that brought thousands of people to the streets of Madrid "serious antidemocratic events that never before happened in the history of our democracy." He added, "Their aim is to influence and pressure the will of voters throughout the day of reflection."

At a polling station in Cozlada, a tight-knit working-class suburb east of Madrid where all four of the attacked trains had passed, there seemed not to be one person who did not know someone who had died.

"Our prime minister has gotten us into a terrible, completely wrong war," Vanessa Bellon, a 23-year-old preschool teacher with a piercing near her lower lip, said as she voted there for the United Left Party. "And because of it, I spent yesterday and today going to funerals. I am thinking of a 3-year-old child at my school who no longer has a mother."

That anger was echoed in the trendy Calle Fuencarral neighborhood of central Madrid. "We've enough of this government," said Nayra Delgado, a 31-year-old documentary filmmaker who voted for the Socialists. "It's too much. They think they are kings in this country."

At El Pozo train station, where one of the attacks occurred, the walls were covered with graffiti that read, "Aznar Killer," and "No to Terrorism." Red candles and bouquets of flowers were haphazardly arranged in tribute to the victims. Just across the street, the polling station was set up in a school, some of whose students had lost parents in the attacks.

"I certainly did not vote for the Popular Party," said a 79-year-old retired carpenter who identified himself only as Julian. "My daughter's hand was cut off, and she almost lost a part of ·her leg. Aznar should come here to see that, to see these people. But he did nothing for us. He did nothing for the poor. He is one who brought us to war. I went through the civil war, and the postwar. But this is worse."

A 26-year-old window frame maker, who identified himself only as David, said he had changed his vote from Popular Party to Socialist because of the bombings and the war in Iraq. "Maybe the Socialists will get our troops out of Iraq, and Al Qaeda will forget about Spain, so we will be less frightened," he said. "A bit of us died in the train."

Addressing both Mr. Aznar and Mr. Rajoy, he said, "I tell them, come to our neighborhoods, we will tell you some things about life, about these poor people who died."

In conservative pockets of the country, people argued that stability, not change, was needed at this time of crisis. In the 12th-century, walled, hilltop city of Avila, the hometown of St. Teresa, voters said they had cast their ballots as they always did—for the Popular Party.

The election of the prime minister involved a complicated process in which voters did not vote for one candidate but for one party list of candidates for deputies in Parliament.

Voters had the choice of 28 party lists, including mainstream parties like the Popular and Socialist parties and tiny ones like the leftist Communist Party of the Peoples of Spain and the rightist Falange, which opposes immigration and supports the memory of the late dictator Franco.

There was little chance of secret ballots; lists were laid out on open tables in polling stations.

——————■——————

With Al Qaeda and other terrorist groups branching out all over the globe, the international community remains perplexed as to how to combat this mounting threat to global peace. The following article from the Beijing Review *examines the spread of terrorism and Al Qaeda's influence within the ever-expanding terrorist network.*

The article also focuses on the new threat of terrorism against Chinese citizens. Since portions of China are situated near countries besieged by terrorism, more and more Chinese citizens are finding themselves in harm's way. This is especially true now that Chinese businesses are more active in seeking foreign trading partners than ever before.

> *To combat the spread of terrorism, China and five*
> *other countries in its region—Russia, Kazakhstan,*
> *Kyrgyzstan, Tajikistan, and Uzbekistan—have formed*
> *the Regional Antiterrorist Structure. This alliance is the*
> *first of its kind in Asia, and it underscores the new sense*
> *of camaraderie between China and its neighbors. —AI*

"Anti-Terrorism Alliance"
by Zhang Lijun
Beijing Review, July 1, 2004

Frequently occurring global terrorist attacks in 2004 have greatly impacted global stability, as well as exerting deep-seated and long-term influences on the future of international politics. The March 11 Madrid bombings, for example, completely changed the political situation in Spain and is believed a major reason for Spanish troops retreating from Iraq.

Nowadays, quite a large number of terrorist attacks are launched by local militia groups, separatists and religious extremists, rather than Al Qaeda members. They follow the deeds of Al Qaeda and mean to achieve their political objectives and enhance their international influence through terrorist attacks. Al Qaeda's terrorist attacks more likely set an example for them. International terrorism has entered a new booming period.

Arc Region Alert

The arc of countries that make up the northeastern part of Africa to the Middle East, Central Asia, South Asia and Southeast Asia occupies only a small area on the world map.

However, this region has caught most of the world's attention. The deep-seated issues such as ethnic contradictions, religious conflicts, border disputes and rampant activities of various terrorists and religious extremists have plunged this region into a state of turmoil. After the September 11 terrorist attacks, the United States has made the region its major anti-terrorist battlefield and launched two large-scale wars in Afghanistan and Iraq, remarkably influencing the stability of the region. Most of the recent globally significant terrorist attacks have taken place in this region. The U.S. Central Intelligence Agency (CIA) estimates that a total of 25,000 various extremists are responsible for terrorist activities worldwide, most of whom are based in this region. These terrorists possess large amounts of capital and modern hi-tech weaponry, posing direct and key threats to the United States.

It is clear Al Qaeda and the remnant forces of the Taliban will never accept defeat and they will launch revenge attacks on the United States and countries that support U.S. anti-terrorist campaigns. They kidnapped and killed U.S. hostages in Saudi Arabia, conducted a series of attacks in Afghanistan and Iraq and attacked Pakistani troops. Meanwhile, separatists, local militia groups and religious extremist forces follow the example of Al Qaeda and conduct attacks for their own interests or to expand their international influence. During three days from March 28 to 30 this year, several terrorist bombings and armed attacks took place in Uzbekistan. Experts believe these attacks were conducted by the Islamic Movement of Uzbekistan (IMU), the largest Islamic extremist organization in Central Asia.

Al Qaeda Effect

Various terrorist and religious extremist forces regard Al Qaeda as their role model and strengthen their connection with Al Qaeda to coordinate their own efforts. Terrorist attacks are developing into a global network.

Before the September 11 attacks, terrorists and religious extremists in the arc region ran rampant. But they only put their emphasis on specific and regional targets, focusing on separatist activities, religious conflicts and vendettas. At that time, they were not interested in establishing Muslim extremist regimes throughout the world and launching all-round terrorist attacks on countries such as the United States and Israel. More importantly, they had little connections with Al Qaeda.

The United States witnessed its darkest day in history on September 11, 2001, when Al Qaeda waged large-scale terrorist attacks on the country. The attacks severely harmed the world superpower.

Terrorists and religious extremists in the arc region were overjoyed by the attacks and took it for granted that terrorist attacks were their best weapons. They started to follow the example of Al Qaeda. After the Afghanistan war, large quantities of Al Qaeda members and remnant forces of the Taliban fled to Central Asian, South Asian and Middle East countries. They formed alliances with local terrorists and religious extremists to retaliate against local governments and people and facilities from western countries, such as the United States.

The CIA revealed that Pakistani President Pervez Musharraf narrowly survived two assassination attempts on December 14 and 25 last year. After investigations and interrogating suspects, Pakistani police believe the two incidents have an international background. C4 plastic explosives, which had never been used in any attacks in the country before, were found in the two attacks. This kind of explosive was used in the Bali bombings in Indonesia in 2002, while the kingpin of the bloody attacks was identified as a head of Al Qaeda–linked Jemaah Islamiya. C4 plastic explosives are also the frequent weapons of Al Qaeda. In September last year, the Qatar-based Al-Jazeera news network broadcast a tape purportedly from Al Qaeda second in command Ayman Al-Zawahri, in which he condemned Musharraf for betraying Islam, appealing to Muslims in Pakistan to rise and overthrow the president.

Meanwhile, terrorists are increasing the scale of their attacks. In the past, it was shocking news if a terrorist attack caused casualties of 10 people. But now, terrorist attacks may take place in succession and it is very common to see an attack claimed dozens of lives. On the other hand, these terrorists have shifted their targets from citizens of the United States and its allies to common locals, UN staff and even citizens from other Third World countries. They mean to bring pressure to bear on governments and influence domestic politics in these countries through damaging the images of governments. Those citizens from other Third World countries and UN staff thus become victims of political and ethnic conflicts in some hotspots.

Reasons for Terror

U.S. policies during its anti-terrorist campaigns are the major reasons to accelerate the instability in the arc region. The campaigns changed the social and economic development of many countries that are at the forefront of anti-terrorist campaigns. In Pakistan and many Southeastern Asian countries, governments were challenged by domestic Islamic forces. Their economic development receded and domestic contradictions became intense, which in turn stimulate Islamic extremist forces to launch anti-governments attacks.

U.S. preemptive strategy in its anti-terrorist campaigns and its ambition to reform the current political systems of some countries also made a great impact on power holders in these countries, especially in the Middle East.

Economic and social problems are another reason for the rise of terrorism. Most of the countries in the arc region are plagued by sluggish economy where a large gap exists between the rich and the poor. Problems such as poverty and unemployment are serious. Even in Saudi Arabia, the richest country in the region, problems such as corruption and wealth gap are alarming. All these provide fertile ground for the development of terrorism. Some unemployed young people who are disenchanted with their lives may be recruited to conduct terrorist activities.

The instability in some countries in the arc region, which saw regime changes as a result of violent changes in their political and social systems, has also given rise to the spread of terrorism. Some enlightened scholars from the United States and western countries stress that the United States should give equal importance to the economic and social problems of the above-mentioned Islamic countries during its anti-terrorist campaigns, such as increasing its assistance to education, health and other sectors of these countries.

Unfortunately, in recent G8 Summit, President Bush put forward his Broader Middle East and North Africa Initiative, putting emphasis still on the political reforms of Middle East countries.

Experts point out that from a long-term angle, the Al Qaeda effect will exert great influence on the entire international situation, posing a threat to the vitality and liability of international anti-terrorist cooperation and the international anti-terrorist alliance. Strong military forces and fierce military mopping up cannot control and eliminate terrorism. On the contrary, it may strengthen it. Eliminating poverty, dispelling injustice and seeking co-development may be the only way to smash terrorism.

China, Another Target for Terrorists?

Few Chinese had imagined they would become targets of terrorist attacks, believing in the shield built on the Chinese Government's insistence on peaceful settlements to all international disputes. However, several terrorist attacks directly against Chinese in recent months have sounded the alarm.

Chinese engineering personnel were on the receiving end of a car bombing on May 3 in the seaport of Gwadar in Pakistan, in which three died and nine were injured. On June 10, a group of terrorists attacked a construction area manned by Chinese workers, killing 11 and injuring four. Different people have different views on these murders. Pakistani scholars say that the terrorist attacks in Gwadar should not be simply considered being launched by religious extremist organizations. They believe a new terrorist organization that premeditated to destroy the Sino-Pakistani friendship is responsible for it. A Chinese reporter stationed in Afghanistan said that the location of the terrorist attack on Chinese workers lies in the northern part of the country, neighboring Tajikistan, an area controlled by Tajik forces of the Northern Alliance where the remnant forces of the Taliban cannot penetrate. It was probably conducted by militants loyal to local warlords. In addition, many local Chinese and experts agree that the Eastern Turkistan Islamic Movement, a Muslim separatist organization, should be held accountable for the massacre.

With the rising of China's overall national strength, an increasing number of Chinese go abroad for investment and project construction. China's neighboring countries are the first step of China's "going global" strategy. The unstable arc region covers a large part of China's neighbors. Chinese has become a new target for terrorists and China should take precautions for future attacks. Meanwhile, China should strengthen communication and coordination with related countries to prevent attacks. Terrorist attacks should not become obstacles to China's "going global" strategy.

During this year's Shanghai Cooperation Organization Summit in Uzbekistan in June, presidents of the organization's six member states—China, Russia, Kazakhstan, Kyrgyzstan, Tajikistan and Uzbekistan—formally launched the Regional Anti-terrorist Structure, and pledged in a joint declaration to cooperate in fighting terrorism and new security threats.

China's domestic terrorist threats are mainly from the East Turkistan separatist forces in Xinjiang Uygur Autonomous Region, which have ganged with international terrorist organizations, such as Al Qaeda. China should learn the U.S. lessons to draft terrorism prevention plans and establish anti-terrorist troops. Meanwhile, measures should be taken to further crack down on international terrorism, national separatism and religious extremism. Terrorist attacks may change the overall strategy of some countries, but it will not influence China's modernization-oriented development path.

———■———

In 2005, the British Broadcasting Corporation (BBC) aired a controversial miniseries entitled The Power of Nightmares, *which examined fear of terrorism throughout the world. In its last installment, the documentary claimed that Al Qaeda was a "paper tiger" inflated by government officials to scare people. The program likened the U.S. government's position against Al Qaeda to that of its position toward the Soviet Union during the Cold War. In other words, the program claimed that the U.S. government exaggerated the threat of an enemy in order to increase its own power and influence.*

The following article comes from the British political magazine New Statesman *and answers the claims set forth by the program* The Power of Nightmares— *claims that have been heavily debated since the program first aired. In the article, author and economist Anthony Giddens examines the differences between the new style of terrorism and the old style of terrorism in order to evaluate the true threat of Al Qaeda. —AI*

"Scaring People May Be the Only Way to Avoid the Risks of New-Style Terrorism"
by Anthony Giddens
New Statesman, January 10, 2005

The current debate about terrorism, including its implications for civil liberties (which were recently highlighted by the law lords' denunciation of British ministers for imprisoning foreign nationals without trial), is vitiated by a failure to distinguish between two types of threat. One type I shall call old-style terrorism—with which we have been familiar for decades. It was practised by groups such as the Red Brigades in Italy or Baader-Meinhof in Germany in the 1960s and 1970s, but it is more commonly associated with nationalist struggles, usually involving "nations without states." It is the sort of conflict associated with Northern Ireland, the Basque country, Quebec or Kashmir.

Such terrorist activity is linked to specific, local objectives. The level of violence is often relatively low—more civilians died on the roads in Northern Ireland during the Troubles than from terrorist violence. Old-style terrorism can become more violent and destructive where it shades into something closer to civil war, as in Israel/Palestine or Sri Lanka.

Old-style terrorism dates back at least as far as the rise of the modern nation state in the 18th century. Globalisation has changed its nature. It can now have far-flung networks of support and finance: the IRA got funding from sympathisers in the US, Libya and other countries, and established links with terrorist groups and guerrillas in central and southern America.

New-style terrorism, however, is directly a child of the global age. Globalisation—meaning the growing interdependence of world society—is not just about the spread of markets and the increasing influence of cross-border financial institutions. It is driven primarily by the development of instantaneous electronic communications and mass transportation; and it is political and cultural, as well as economic.

Al-Qaeda and its activities form a prototypical example of new-style terrorism, but al-Qaeda is by no means the only group of its kind. Mary Kaldor, of the Centre for the Study of Global Governance at the London School of Economics, has described al-Qaeda as being run in some ways as if it were a non-governmental organisation such as Oxfam or Friends of the Earth. The analogy cannot be stretched too far because NGOs are open and legitimate, while new-style terrorist groups are covert and illegal. Yet the similarities are striking. Both al-Qaeda-type organisations and NGOs are highly decentralised. They are loose networks, driven by a sense of mission that holds together disparate groups or cells across the world, which quite often act semi-autonomously. Both deploy up-to-date communications technologies to co-ordinate their actions and to promote their messages. They have home bases, but these are in principle mutable and diverse. The home bases of new-style terrorist groups are in failing states, but they may also get covert support from governments elsewhere.

The goals of the new-style terrorists are not local, but more far-reaching. Al-Qaeda's aims, as expressed in Osama Bin Laden's proclamations, are truly geopolitical. Bin Laden

wants to see the "Crusader-Jewish alliance" driven out of
Arabia, and ultimately proposes the re-creation of a
caliphate running from Pakistan through to North Africa
and southern Spain.

This is the first difference between new and old terrorists.
The aims of the former are wider, but also vaguer, than those
of the latter. That is why negotiation, much less settlement, is
generally impossible. The second important difference concerns organisational capacity. New systems of communication,
allied to rapid travel, allow groups to organise at a distance
and to co-ordinate terrorist actions. The third difference is
ruthlessness. New-style terrorists are prepared to kill thousands, even millions.

The fourth difference is weaponry. The internet allows
anyone with the requisite technical knowledge and resources
to develop weapons of high destructive potential. And following the collapse of the Soviet Union, large amounts of
weaponry are circulating through the illegal global arms trade.
Thousands of nuclear weapons and stocks of weapons-usable
materials are held in insecure silos in Russia, vulnerable to
theft by those who might sell them to terrorists. Enough
nuclear material to build 20 medium-sized nuclear weapons is
known to have gone missing in Russia.

The combination of organisational capacity and ruthlessness made 9/11 a landmark in the history of terrorism: it was
the first successful large-scale attack on the US mainland
since the British invasion from Canada in 1814; and it could
have been even more destructive than it was. The hijacked
planes were aimed at the three centres of US power: financial,
military and political. If the twin towers had collapsed straight

away, 50,000 people, instead of 3,000, could have been killed. Flight 77 would have done more damage if it had hit the Pentagon more centrally. And the fourth plane—aimed at either the Capitol or the White House—fell short of its target thanks to the bravery of passengers on board.

It is now commonly argued, especially on the left, that governments overhype the risks from terrorism, and that al-Qaeda is something of a paper tiger. This view was put forward last year, for instance, in two programmes in the BBC series The Power of Nightmares, directed by Adam Curtis. Al-Qaeda, Curtis argued, does not really exist: western intelligence agencies and politicians have turned a few, widely scattered terrorist incidents into a sinister global conspiracy. Two US experts on terrorism, Adam Dolnik and Kimberly McCloud, similarly claim that it is time we "defused the widespread image of al-Qaeda as a ubiquitous, super-organised terror network and call it as it is: a loose collection of groups and individuals that doesn't even call itself al-Qaeda." According to them, Osama Bin Laden never spoke of "al-Qaeda" before 9/11; it had only cropped up, in a marginal way, in the pronouncements of those around him. US intelligence agencies first used "al-Qaeda" in a generic fashion after the 1998 embassy bombings in Kenya and Tanzania. Only later was the title appropriated by the terrorist groups themselves.

It is indeed mistaken to suppose that al-Qaeda is a highly organised global machine capable of wreaking havoc wherever its leaders decide; rather, it is a network of various types of group, some more effective and menacing than others. Yet it is equally mistaken to underplay the threat from these. After all, 9/11 did happen—and it involved careful planning and sophisticated logistics.

Bin Laden and his immediate associates are almost certainly less of a danger than they were—because of the military intervention in Afghanistan, not because their capacities at the time were exaggerated. Their warriors were forced to leave their bases and many were killed in the fighting. At least one top commander, Muhammad Atef, died in the air strikes. Three other senior leaders were captured in Pakistan, including Khalid Sheikh Mohammed, who was allegedly the prime figure behind the 9/11 attacks.

Al-Qaeda probably retains "sleepers" in western countries, over and above the cells broken up by police in the US, UK, France, Spain, Germany and elsewhere. There are other terrorist organisations that share the same fundamentalist outlook as al-Qaeda and have connections with it, such as the Egyptian Islamic Jihad, the Islamic Army of Aden (which originates in the Yemen) or the Islamic Movement of Uzbekistan.

The recent report on homeland security in the United States, produced by a task force guided by Richard A. Clarke, distinguishes three "concentric circles" of international jihadist terrorism. Al-Qaeda is the "inner circle," with an estimated membership today of between 400 and 2,000 activists. In the second circle are numerous further terror groups, with between 50,000 and 200,000 members. The outer circle comprises jihadist sympathisers in the global Islamic community, numbering upwards of 200 million.

Those who play down the importance of terrorist threats, or who speak of a gratuitous "politics of fear," are apt to say: "There hasn't been another 9/11; we were told that a terrorist attack on London was almost inevitable, but nothing has happened. Why were you scaring everybody without good reason?" This view is specious, for two reasons. The first concerns the phenomenology of risk. In order to get people to take a risk seriously and respond in the right way, they have to be told how potentially dangerous it is. If the threat does not materialise, those who spoke of it are likely to be accused of scaremongering. But scaring people—getting them to see that the risk is real—may be the very condition of minimising or avoiding danger. One weekend in 2003, the Prime Minister, after receiving intelligence information, decided to surround Heathrow with troops. He was criticised for scaremongering. Yet his actions may have stopped a terrorist attack.

The second reason why it is wrong to talk of the "politics of fear" is specific to new-style terrorism. It is simply the magnitude of the dangers involved. The chances of a terrorist attack on London that kills thousands may be slight, especially considering the precautions in place. It is now difficult to implement attacks using planes. It is hard to deploy chemical and biological weapons on a large-scale basis against civilians. A "dirty bomb"—almost certain to be set off some time, somewhere—would cause widespread panic, but its lethal range is limited. There is no evidence so far of nuclear weapons or materials falling into the hands of new-style terrorists, although no one really knows.

However, the truth is that a highly destructive strike is no longer just a hypothetical possibility. The consequences of old-style terrorism may be horrific, but can be weathered. The same is not true of a large-scale terrorist attack: just one episode could be devastating, and one involving a nuclear device cataclysmic. The IRA's warning, after the bombing of the Conservative Party conference in Brighton in 1984, that "we only have to be lucky once; you will have to be lucky always" has a new and more acute meaning in the age of new-style terrorism. We have to avoid even a single successful attack; but the longer we do so, the more, perversely, critics will proclaim that we are all being scared unnecessarily.

The left has to adjust its attitudes towards terrorism, just as it had to adjust them towards crime. It won't do to say that there are no serious threats. It won't do to blame the troubles of the world on George W. Bush or the Iraq war. It is no good pretending that there aren't problems in reconciling civil liberties with adequate protection and security. It is not wrong to say that we have to deal with the social conditions that have helped to produce new-style terrorism—poverty and unemployment, schisms between the Islamic world and the west, the situation in Israel/Palestine. And it is certainly right to say that we need urgent measures to halt further nuclear proliferation.

But as with crime, we cannot think only of the underlying conditions. New-style terrorists are by no means always drawn from the ranks of the dispossessed; and their aims, as in the case of al-Qaeda, may be primarily religious and strategic. We have to respond to the dangers they pose in the here and now.

TIMELINE

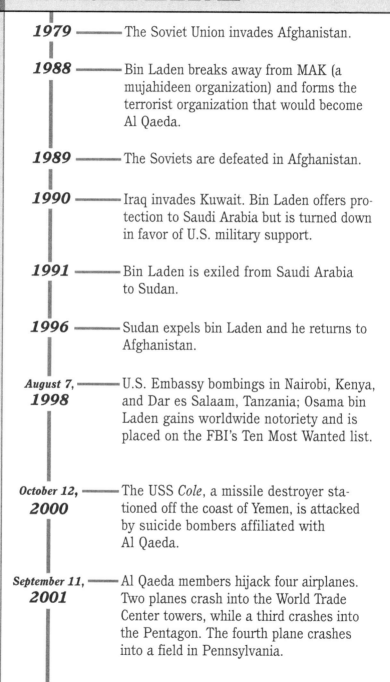

1979 — The Soviet Union invades Afghanistan.

1988 — Bin Laden breaks away from MAK (a mujahideen organization) and forms the terrorist organization that would become Al Qaeda.

1989 — The Soviets are defeated in Afghanistan.

1990 — Iraq invades Kuwait. Bin Laden offers protection to Saudi Arabia but is turned down in favor of U.S. military support.

1991 — Bin Laden is exiled from Saudi Arabia to Sudan.

1996 — Sudan expels bin Laden and he returns to Afghanistan.

August 7, 1998 — U.S. Embassy bombings in Nairobi, Kenya, and Dar es Salaam, Tanzania; Osama bin Laden gains worldwide notoriety and is placed on the FBI's Ten Most Wanted list.

October 12, 2000 — The USS *Cole*, a missile destroyer stationed off the coast of Yemen, is attacked by suicide bombers affiliated with Al Qaeda.

September 11, 2001 — Al Qaeda members hijack four airplanes. Two planes crash into the World Trade Center towers, while a third crashes into the Pentagon. The fourth plane crashes into a field in Pennsylvania.

October 2001 — The United States invades Afghanistan. The war on terror begins.

October 12, 2002 — A nightclub in Bali, Indonesia, is bombed. More than 200 people are killed in the blast. The attack is linked to Al Qaeda.

March 1, 2003 — Khalid Shaikh Mohammed is captured by the Pakistani intelligence agency, ISI, and is taken into U.S. custody.

March 11, 2004 — A subway in Madrid, Spain, is bombed, killing 200 and wounding more than 1,000. Evidence points to Al Qaeda involvement in the attacks.

July 22, 2004 — The 9/11 Commission releases a final report that names Al Qaeda and Osama bin Laden as the perpetrators of the 9/11 attacks on the United States.

October 29, 2004 — Footage of bin Laden giving a speech to the United States is released by Aljazeera. Bin Laden admits responsibility for the 9/11 attacks for the first time.

November 2, 2004 — George W. Bush is elected to a second term as president of the United States.

July 7, 2005 — Four suicide bombers detonate bombs on subway trains and a bus in London, killing more than fifty commuters. Authorities suspect that Al Qaeda was involved in the attacks.

FOR MORE INFORMATION

Central Intelligence Agency
Office of Public Affairs
Washington, DC 20505
(703) 482-0623
Web site: http://www.cia.gov

Council on Foreign Relations
The Harold Pratt House
58 East 68th Street
New York, NY 10021
(212) 434-9400
Web site: http://www.cfr.org

Terrorism Research Center
5765 F- Burke Center Parkway
PBM 331
Burke, VA 22015
(877) 635-0816
Web site: http://www.terrorism.com

U.S. Department of Homeland Security
Washington, DC 20528
(202) 282-8000
Web site: http://www.dhs.gov/dhspublic

U.S. Department of State
Office of the Coordinator for Counterterrorism
Office of Public Affairs, Room 2509
2201 C Street NW
Washington, DC 20520
(202) 647-4000
Web site: http://www.state.gov/s/ct

Web Sites

Due to the changing nature of Internet links, the Rosen
Publishing Group, Inc., has developed an online list of Web
sites related to the subject of this book. This site is updated
regularly. Please use this link to access the list:

http://www.rosenlinks.com/canf/alqa

FOR FURTHER READING

Burke, Jason. *Al-Qaeda: Casting a Shadow of Terror*. London, England: I.B. Tauris, 2003.

Clarke, Richard A. *Against All Enemies: Inside America's War on Terror*. New York, NY: The Free Press, 2004.

Coll, Steve. *Ghost Wars: The Secret History of the CIA, Afghanistan, and bin Laden, from the Soviet Invasion to September 10, 2001*. New York, NY: Penguin: 2004.

Gunaratna, Rohan. *Inside Al Qaeda: Global Network of Terror*. New York, NY: Columbia University Press, 2002.

Hersh, Seymour M. *Chain of Command: The Road from 9/11 to Abu Ghraib*. New York, NY: Harper Collins, 2004.

Kepel, Gilles. *Jihad: The Trail of Political Islam*. Cambridge, MA: Harvard University Press, 2002.

Murdico, Suzanne J. *The Gulf War*. New York, NY: Rosen Publishing Group, 2004.

National Commission on Terrorist Attacks Upon the United States. *The 9/11 Commission Report*. New York, NY: W. W. Norton and Company, 2004.

Randal, Jonathan. *Osama: The Making of a Terrorist*. New York, NY: Knopf, 2004.

Rashid, Ahmed. *Jihad: The Rise of Militant Islam in Central Asia*. New York, NY: Penguin, 2003.

ANNOTATED BIBLIOGRAPHY

Aljazeera.net. "Excerpts from Usama bin Ladin's Speech." October 29, 2004 (http://english.aljazeera.net/NR/exeres/ 8BAF429F-BADD-40E2-AD66-712FCF7D7A95.htm). This speech by Osama bin Laden is often referred to as the "October surprise." It initially aired on the Aljazeera television network.

Benjamin, Daniel and Steven Simon. *The Age of Sacred Terror.* New York, NY: Random House, 2002. This excerpt from the chapter entitled "Raiders on the Path of God" details the rise of the Taliban in Afghanistan.
From THE AGE OF SACRED TERROR by Daniel Benjamin and Steven Simon, copyright © 2002 by Daniel Benjamin and Steven Simon. Used by permission of Random House, Inc.

Bergen, Peter. *Holy War, Inc.* New York, NY: The Free Press, 2001. Bergen is a terrorism analyst for CNN and professor of International Studies at Johns Hopkins University.
Reprinted and edited with the permission of The Free Press, a Division of Simon & Schuster Adult Publishing Group, from HOLY WAR, INC.: Inside the Secret World of Osama bin Laden by Peter L. Bergen. Copyright © 2001 by Peter L. Bergen. All rights reserved.

Bergen, Peter. "The Long Hunt for Osama." *Atlantic Monthly*, October 2004, Vol. 294, No. 3, pp. 88–100. In this excerpt, Bergen, one of the few Western journalists to have met Osama bin Laden, describes the United States' pursuit of bin Laden through the rugged landscapes of Afghanistan and Pakistan.
"The Long Hunt for Osama" by Peter Bergen. Copyright © 2004 by Peter Bergen. Originally published in The Atlantic Monthly. *Reprinted by permission of the author.*

Burke, Jason. "Hidden Letters Reveal Dark Secrets of School for Terror." *Observer*, November 25, 2001. In this selection,

a journalist travels to the eastern Afghan city of Khowst and visits an abandoned Al Qaeda training camp.
Reprinted with permission. Copyright Guardian Newspapers Limited 2001

Carr, Caleb. "The Art of Knowing the Enemy." *New York Times*, December 21, 2001. Carr is best known for his books of fiction, including *The Alienist*. He also writes frequently on politics and military issues, and is a contributing editor of *MHG: The Quarterly Journal of Military History*.
Copyright © 2001 by Caleb Carr. Reprinted by permission of William Morris Agency, LLC on behalf of the author. Originally published in the New York Times.

Corn, David. "Al Qaeda Disconnect." *Nation*, July 5, 2004, Vol. 279, No. 1, pp. 4–5. Corn is the Washington editor of *The Nation* and author of *The Lies of George W. Bush*. He is also a frequent contributor to Fox News Channel and National Public Radio.
"Al Qaeda Disconnect" by David Corn. Reprinted with permission from the July 5, 2004, issue of The Nation. For subscription information, call 1-800-333-8536. Portions of each week's Nation magazine can be accessed at http://www.thenation.com.

Cullison, Alan. "Inside Al-Qaeda's Hard Drive." *Atlantic Monthly*, September 2004, Vol. 294, No. 2, pp. 55–70. Cullison is a Moscow correspondent for *The Wall Street Journal* and a Nieman fellow at Harvard University.
Reprinted with permission from Alan Cullison.

David, Peter. "In the Name of Islam." *Economist*, September 13, 2003, Vol. 368, No. 8341, pp. 3–4. This article is part of a special section within the *Economist* entitled "A Survey of Islam and the West." The special section consists of seven articles discussing political, cultural, and economic developments in the Muslim world.
© 2003 The Economist Newspaper Ltd. All rights reserved. Reprinted with permission. Further reproduction prohibited. www.economist.com.

Dobbs, Michael. "Inside the Mind of Osama bin Laden." *Washington Post*, September 20, 2001. Dobbs is a reporter

for the *Washington Post* and the author of several books, including *Down with Big Brother*, a runner-up for the 1997 PEN Award for nonfiction.
© 2001, The Washington Post, *reprinted with permission.*

Giddens, Anthony. "Scaring People May Be the Only Way to Avoid the Risks of New-Style Terrorism." *New Statesman*, January 10, 2005, Vol. 18, No. 840, pp. 29–31. Giddens is the director of the London School of Economics and Political Sciences. He is the author of thirty-four books published in twenty-nine languages.
© *New Statesman. All rights reserved.*

Gordon, Michael R. "U.S. Tries to Sway Worldwide Opinion in Favor of War." *New York Times*, November 6, 2001. This article reports on the American efforts to increase global support of the military campaign in Afghanistan.
Copyright © 2001 by The New York Times Co. Reprinted with permission.

Johnston, David, and David E. Sanger. "New Leaders Are Emerging for Al Qaeda." *New York Times*, August 10, 2004. This article reports on how the arrest of Mohammed Naeem Noor Khan, an Al Qaeda computer expert, has provided U.S. intelligence officials with information concerning the new leadership of the organization.
Copyright © 2004 by The New York Times Co. Reprinted with permission.

Kaplan, David E., and Kevin Whitelaw. "Terror's New Soldiers." *U.S. News and World Report*, November 1, 2004, Vol. 137, No. 15, pp. 34–35. This cover story details the rise of new terrorist groups after 9/11 and questions the success of the war on terrorism.
Copyright 2004. U.S. News & World Report, L.P. Reprinted with permission.

McCarthy, Andrew C. "Three Years and Counting." *National Review*, December 13, 2004, Vol. 56, No. 23, pp. 34–36.

From 1993 to 1996, Andrew C. McCarthy led the prosecution for the United States against the jihad organization of Sheik Omar Abdel Rahman. Currently, he is a senior fellow for the Foundation for the Defense of Democracies.
© 2004 by National Review, Inc., 215 Lexington Avenue, New York, NY 10016. Reprinted by permission.

Ratnesar, Romesh. "Al-Qaeda's New Proving Ground." *Time*, October 28, 2002, Vol. 160, No. 18, pp. 35–36. Ratnesar provides an in-depth report of terrorism in Indonesia, shortly after the bombing of a nightclub on the island of Bali.
© 2002 TIME Inc. Reprinted by permission.

Sciolino, Elaine. "Following Attacks, Spain's Governing Party is Beaten." *New York Times*, March 15, 2004. Elaine Sciolino is a senior writer for the *New York Times* and author of *Persian Mirrors: The Elusive Face of Iran*.
Copyright © 2004 by The New York Times Co. Reprinted with permission.

Thomas, Evan. "Al Qaeda in America: The Enemy Within." *Newsweek*, June 23, 2003, Vol. 141, No. 25, p. 40. This article discusses the capture of Khalid Shaikh Mohammed and the extent to which his confessions and the contents of his computer have provided government officials with a better understanding of Al Qaeda activity within the United States.
From Newsweek, 6/23/2003 © 2003 Newsweek, Inc. All rights reserved. Reprinted by permission.

Whitelaw, Kevin. "Going After the Bad Guys." *U.S. News and World Report*, September 14, 2001, Vol. 131, No. 11, p. 32. Written three days after 9/11, this article looks at the massive investigation into who was responsible for the attacks.
Copyright 2001 U.S. News & World Report, L.P. Reprinted with permission.

"Wrath of God." *Time Asia*, January 11, 1999, Vol. 153, No. 1. This interview with Osama bin Laden took place before

9/11 and allows a glimpse into the mind of the world's most wanted terrorist.

Zakaria, Fareed. "Bin Laden's Bad Bet." *Newsweek*, September 11, 2002, Vol. 140, No. 11, pp. 34–35. Zakaria's most recent book is *The Future of Freedom: Illiberal Democracy at Home and Abroad* (2003). He is also the author of *From Wealth to Power*, a study of America's role on the world stage.
From Newsweek, *9/11/2002 © 2002 Newsweek, Inc. All rights reserved. Reprinted by permission.*

Zhang Lijun. "Anti-Terrorism Alliance." *Beijing Review*, July 1, 2004, Vol. 47, No. 26, pp. 10–13. Zhang Lijun is an assistant researcher with the China Institute of International Studies.
Reprinted with permission from Beijing Review.

INDEX

A

Abd al-Wahhab, Muhammad ibn, 61, 64
Abu Ghaith, Sulaiman, 85
Afghan Arabs, 16–18, 19, 42, 43
Afghanistan
  rise of Taliban in, 38–43
  Soviet invasion of/war in, 5–6, 9, 10–19, 37, 46, 69, 71
  U.S. invasion of/war in, 7, 31–32, 33, 50, 51, 63, 123, 124–128, 154, 165
Aljazeera, 80, 124, 125, 127, 156
anti-Americanism, 8, 13, 27, 34, 52, 63, 96
Ashcroft, John, 20, 23, 55, 115, 138
Atef, Muhammad, 104–105, 106, 165
Atta, Mohamed, 45, 56, 82, 130, 131
Azhar, Maulana Masood, 87
Aznar, Jose Maria, 146, 147, 148, 149, 150, 151
Azzam, Abdullah, 5, 13–16, 18

B

Bali, Indonesia, 2002 nightclub bombing, 7, 112, 141, 142–146, 156
Bearden, Milt, 17, 52
Beers, Charlotte, 125
Beit al-Ansar (House of the Supporters), 13, 18

Benjamin, Daniel, 37
Bergen, Peter, 9, 72, 83
bin Attash, Walid Muhammad Salih (Khallad), 34, 88
bin Laden, Osama
  background of, 5–7
  hunt for, 83, 84–96
  interview with Rahimullah Yusufzai, 74–80
  and leadership of Al Qaeda, 6, 7, 33, 36, 50
  and September 11, 2001, attacks, 6, 7, 20, 21, 22, 23, 25, 28, 36, 66, 80, 81–83
  and Soviet invasion of Afghanistan 9, 12–14, 16, 18, 19, 37
  and the Taliban, 6–7, 23, 37, 41–42, 43, 73, 78, 94, 98, 99, 100, 102, 130
  uncovered correspondence of, 97, 99–100, 108–111
  and U.S. Embassy bombings, 21, 24, 45, 66, 68, 73, 74–75
  videotapes of, 55, 56, 72, 80, 81–83, 85, 127
  worldview and ideology of, 6, 27, 58, 62, 67–72, 72–73, 162–163
Black, Cofer, 52, 89–90
Blitzer, Robert, 21
Burke, Jason, 43–44
Bush, George W./Bush administration, 23, 31, 33, 51, 52,

About the Editor

April Isaacs received an MFA in nonfiction writing from New School University in 2004. Shortly after the September 11, 2001, attacks on the World Trade Center, Isaacs moved to New York's Financial District, only blocks away from Ground Zero, where she witnessed the aftermath of the attacks on a daily basis. The events of 9/11 deeply impacted her life and motivated her to learn more about terrorism and the Al Qaeda terrorist network. She currently lives in New York City, where she works as an editor and writer.

Photo Credits

Cover, p.1: © Getty Images.

Designer: Gene Mollica; Series Editor: Brian Belval
Photo Research: Gene Mollica